The ASTRONAUT Training Book for Kids

The ASTRONAUT Training Book for Kids

KIM LONG

LODESTAR BOOKS
Dutton   New York

Library of Congress Cataloging-in-Publication Data

Long, Kim.
   The astronaut training book for kids / Kim Long.
      p. cm.
   "Lodestar Books."
   Includes bibliographies and index.
   Summary: Discusses the history and future potential of astronautics and provides
information about the education and training necessary for a career in this field.
    ISBN 0-525-67296-6
    1. Astronautics—Vocational guidance—Juvenile literature. [1. Astronautics—
Vocational guidance. 2. Vocational guidance.]
I. Title.
TL793.L66 1990   89-34668
629.45′0023—dc20   CIP
                                                       AC

Published in the United States by Lodestar Books, an affiliate of Dutton Children's Books,
a division of Penguin Books USA Inc.

Published simultaneously in Canada by Fitzhenry & Whiteside Limited, Toronto

Editor: Rosemary Brosnan   Designer: Marilyn Granald, LMD
Printed in the U.S.A.   First Edition   10 9 8 7 6 5 4 3 2 1

this book is dedicated to
the next generation of astronauts

Contents

Acknowledgments

This book was prepared with information and assistance from many people and organizations. Thanks to:

Pat Wagner and Leif Smith (Office for Open Network, Denver, Colorado); Dr. Randall Lockwood (Humane Society of the U.S.); Denver Public Library; Kathleen Cain (Front Range Community College Library, Westminster, Colorado); Dan Michaels (Colorado Science Olympiad); Elmer Bernath (Junior Academy of Sciences); Junior Engineering Technical Society; Dr. Daniel Caldwell (Junior Science and Humanities Symposium); Mary Taylor (Denver Public Schools); Odyssey of the Mind; Betsy Wright (Denver Public Schools); President's Council on Physical Fitness; Lisa Ferreria (National Science Teachers Association); Quantum Link; Greg Walz-Chojnacki (*Odyssey* magazine); American Camping Association; Broderbund Software (San Rafael, California); Electronic Arts (San Mateo, California); Rich Baker (Compuserve, Columbus, Ohio); Nancy Beckman (The Source, McLean, Virginia); Science Service (Washington, D.C.); Linda Durham (National Association of Secondary School Principals); Professional Engineers of Colorado; Ellen Christie (Girl Scouts of the U.S.A.); National 4-H Council; Len Streeter (Shuttle Camp 2001, Alamagordo, New Mexico); Vernier Software; Chris Ronningen-Fenrich (Grolier Electronic Publishing); Jim Poindexter; Chuck Biggs; Lou Parker (NASA Johnson Space Center); Larry Sessions (Denver Museum of Natural History); Kathy and Tim Havens (S & S Optika, Denver, Colorado); David Eagle (Science Software, Littleton, Colorado); Jill Steele (National Space Society, Denver, Colorado); John Rossi (Western Telecommunications, Inc., Englewood, Colorado); Dr. John Akey (U.S. Space Foundation, Colorado Springs, Colorado); Greg Maryniak (Space Studies Institute); International Aerospace Hall of Fame (San Diego, California); Ellen Walker (Kansas Cosmosphere, Hutchinson, Kansas); Aerospace America; Steve Cobaugh (United States Space Education Association); Young Astronaut Council; Dr. Kerry Joels (Challenger Foundation); Trudy Bell (IEEE); Boy Scouts of America; Michael Dell and Jeff Scheuren (University of Colorado Small Business Assistance Center); Pat Miller (National Association of Model Rocketry); Mary Roberts (Estes Rockets); Ken Goss (Aerospace Education Foundation); American Astronautical Society; American Astronomical Society; American Institute of Aeronautics and Astronautics; Association of Lunar and Planetary Observers; Ted Everts (Association of Space Explorers); Mike Schrier; Noel Bullock (Civil Air Patrol, Aerospace Education); Carmella Tetta (Institute of Electrical and Electronics Engineers); Elizabeth Karpiej (International Amateur Radio Union); Tod Holly (International Space University); Students for the Exploration and Development of Space; Spaceweek (Houston, Texas); Diane Riley (National Mathematics League); Leslie Collins (National Society of Professional Engineers).

The ASTRONAUT Training Book for Kids

Introduction

> **WANTED :** Dedicated
>   workers for exciting jobs
>   in space.
> Apply to:
> Astronaut Recruiting
> Mail Code AP-4
> NASA—Johnson Space
>   Center
> Houston, Texas 77058

So you want to be an astronaut. Being an astronaut may be the most exciting job on earth, or above it. Your parents probably wish they could be astronauts, too, but they may already be too old. When they were your age, flying in space was still a new adventure, and only a few special test pilots got picked to join NASA for space flights.

Between then and now, a whole new era of space exploration has begun, and the future will bring even more development. There will be many new jobs for astronauts by the time you become an adult. And there will also be many other space enthusiasts like you, so the competition to be chosen as an astronaut will be tough.

This book is intended to give you a head start on a career in space. Are there any magic formulas or tricks? No—you will have to work hard, learn a lot of math and science, and develop good study habits if you want to succeed.

You don't have to read this book from front to back. You can jump in anywhere it is interesting to you. Some chapters have MISSIONS, which describe important areas of interest for a would-be astronaut. If you find something that is exciting, go ahead and do it. It is easier to get ideas, answers, or enthusiasm while you are doing something than if you wait for them to come to you. You can start with lists of activities, groups to join, and books and magazines to read—or maybe you'll think of something even better.

Good luck, don't give up, see you in orbit.

1

Why Space?

What career should you choose? You could be a doctor, a lawyer, a fire fighter, or almost anything. All of these occupations, and most others, are pursued on earth. If you become an astronaut, you will be spending part of your working life away from earth, in space. Why would people want to leave this planet?

- Many scientific experiments can only be done in space. The absence of gravity and the ready supply of vacuum can be used to perform research that can't be done on earth, or at least not as well as in space. For astronomers, there is no atmospheric distortion to diminish observations of faraway celestial objects. For geologists, there is the opportunity to study details of the earth's surface from above.
- Many new products can be made in space. These include crystals, computer chips, metal alloys, and pharmaceutical drugs. Using the advantages of micro-gravity, scientists can produce these and many other items for use on earth or for making more advanced space vehicles.
- New supplies of raw materials, such as minerals and metallic ores on the moon, the planets, and the asteroids, are waiting for us. Mining these can help conserve the limited resources of earth. Titanium, for instance, is a valuable substance because it is very important in the production of strong, lightweight steel, but there is not enough to meet the demand. On the moon, the Apollo

astronauts discovered large quantities of it. Another important resource of space is the sun's intense solar energy. This can be used to provide energy for manufacturing and living both in space and on earth, by using microwave beams to transfer it from collection satellites to earth-based power stations.

- Finally, there is an age-old urge in humans to explore. People have investigated almost every place on earth, but space is still a huge and unknown territory, waiting to be discovered. Maybe the biggest reason to be an astronaut is to be a modern explorer, to find out what is out there, to be the first to uncover the mysteries of space.

2

The History of People in Space

The first object to be flown into space was the Sputnik I, a satellite launched by Russia on October 4, 1957. The first living creature to reach space was Laika, a dog on board the Soviet satellite Sputnik II, which was launched on November 3, 1957.

The Soviet Union beat the United States in this race to reach outer space, but the competition helped speed up America's effort to design and build rockets and satellites. The first U.S. satellite in space was the Explorer I, launched on January 31, 1958. Rapid advancements quickly followed this successful effort, and an American space vehicle, the Pioneer 4, reached the moon in March 1959.

One year earlier, in 1958, the National Aeronautics and Space Administration (NASA) was created to oversee the space program of the United States. One of NASA's first goals was to put a person into space, and this was accomplished on May 5, 1961. However, the Soviets were first again, because they had launched their own cosmonaut into space a week earlier.

In the 1960s, the U.S. and the U.S.S.R. launched dozens of people into space and developed the basic programs for orbiting humans around the earth. The space race became a contest to see which country could accomplish new space adventures first, and the U.S., after its late start, moved ahead in most areas.

On July 20, 1969, the U.S. was the first country to put a person on the moon. In six different expeditions to the lunar surface, twelve

American astronauts landed on the moon and performed hundreds of experiments. Some of the moon rocks that were brought back are still being tested in laboratories.

Meanwhile, the Soviets were concentrating on putting more people into orbit around the earth, and leaving them in orbit for longer periods of time. Both the U.S. and U.S.S.R. experimented with small orbiting space stations, and in 1975 the two countries cooperated in a joint adventure when the American Apollo 18 docked with the Soviet Soyuz 19.

HISTORICAL TIMETABLE OF MANNED SPACE TRAVEL

Date	Crew	Country	Mission	Duration of Flight
April 12, 1961 *(Gagarin is first man in space)*	Gagarin	U.S.S.R.	Vostok 1	1 hour, 48 minutes
May 5, 1961 *(Shepard is first American in space—shortest spaceflight on record)*	Shepard	U.S.A.	Freedom 7	15 minutes, 30 seconds
August 6, 1961 *(first flight longer than one day)*	Titov	U.S.S.R.	Vostok 2	25 hours, 18 minutes
February 20, 1962 *(Glenn is first American to orbit the earth)*	Glenn	U.S.A.	Friendship 7	4 hours, 55 minutes
June 16, 1963 *(Tereshkova is first woman in space)*	Tereshkova	U.S.S.R.	Vostok 6	70 hours, 50 minutes
October 12, 1964 *(first three-man crew in space)*	Komarov Feoktistov Yegorov	U.S.S.R.	Voskhod 1	24 hours, 17 minutes
March 18, 1965 *(Leonov is first person to walk in space)*	Bel'yayev Leonov	U.S.S.R.	Voskhod 2	26 hours, 2 minutes
June 3, 1965 *(first two-man American spaceflight)*	McDivitt White	U.S.A.	Gemini 4	97 hours, 56 minutes

HISTORICAL TIMETABLE OF MANNED SPACE TRAVEL *(continued)*

Date	Crew	Country	Mission	Duration of Flight
December 21, 1968	Borman Lovell Anders	U.S.A.	Apollo 8	147 hours, 1 minute
(first manned flight around the moon)				
July 16, 1969	Armstrong Aldrin Collins	U.S.A.	Apollo 11	195 hours, 19 minutes
(Armstrong is first man to walk on the moon)				
July 26, 1971	Scott Irwin Worden	U.S.A.	Apollo 15	295 hours, 12 minutes
(Lunar Rover first used on the moon)				
May 25, 1973	Conrad Kerwin Weitz	U.S.A.	Skylab 2	672 hours, 50 minutes
(first Americans in orbiting space station)				
November 16, 1973	Carr Gibson Pogue	U.S.A.	Skylab 4	2017 hours, 16 minutes
(longest U.S. spaceflight)				
July 15, 1975	Leonov Kubasov	U.S.S.R.	Soyuz 19	142 hours, 31 minutes
	Stafford Brand Slayton	U.S.A.	Apollo-Soyuz	217 hours, 28 minutes
(Soyuz 19 and Apollo 18 dock)				
December 10, 1977	Romanenko Grechko	U.S.S.R.	Soyuz 26	2898 hours, 6 minutes
(new endurance record set for time in space)				
April 12, 1981	Young Crippen	U.S.A.	STS-1	54 hours, 21 minutes
(first test flight of Space Shuttle Columbia)				

Astronaut Alan B. Shepard, Jr., commander of the Apollo 14 mission, plants the American flag on the moon during an extravehicular activity excursion. NASA

Launch of the Space Shuttle Discovery
LOCKHEED MISSILES & SPACE COMPANY, INC.

Astronauts John
Young and Robert
Crippen aboard the
Columbia, the first
space shuttle to orbit
the earth   NASA

The Space Shuttle
Atlantis, moments
before lift-off   NASA

HISTORICAL TIMETABLE OF MANNED SPACE TRAVEL (*continued*)

Date	Crew	Country	Mission	Duration of Flight
May 13, 1982	Berezovoy Lebedev	U.S.S.R.	Soyuz T-5	2549 hours, 6 minutes
(*Salyut 7 space station first occupied*)				
November 11, 1982	Brand Overmyer Allen Lenoir	U.S.A.	STS-5	122 hours, 14 minutes
(*first commercial flight for a space shuttle*)				
April 4, 1983	Weitz Bobko Peterson Musgrave	U.S.A.	STS-6	120 hours, 24 minutes
(*first flight of Space Shuttle Challenger; first space walk from space shuttle*)				
June 18, 1983	Crippen Hauck Fabian Thagard Ride	U.S.A.	STS-7 (Challenger)	146 hours, 24 minutes
(*Ride is first American woman in space*)				
August 30, 1983	Truly Brandenstein Bluford Gardner Thornton	U.S.A.	STS-8 (Challenger)	145 hours, 9 minutes
(*first night launch and landing of space shuttle*)				

HISTORICAL TIMETABLE OF MANNED SPACE TRAVEL *(continued)*

Date	Crew	Country	Mission	Duration of Flight
November 28, 1983	Young Shaw Garriott Parker Lichtenberg Merbold	U.S.A.	STS-9 (Columbia)	247 hours, 47 minutes
(first flight of Spacelab 1)				
February 3, 1984	Brand Gibson McCandless Stewart McNair	U.S.A.	STS 41-B (Challenger)	191 hours, 16 minutes
(first use of Manned Maneuvering Unit (MMU) for space walk)				
February 8, 1984	Kizim Solovyev Atkov	U.S.S.R.	Soyuz T-10	1510 hours, 43 minutes
(longest manned spaceflight to date)				
April 6, 1984	Crippen Scobee Nelson Hart van Hoften	U.S.A.	STS 41-C (Challenger)	167 hours, 40 minutes
(first satellite repaired in orbit)				
July 17, 1984	Dzhanibekov Savitskaya Volk	U.S.S.R.	Soyuz T-12	283 hours, 14 minutes
(Savitskaya is first woman to walk in space)				

HISTORICAL TIMETABLE OF MANNED SPACE TRAVEL *(continued)*

Date	Crew	Country	Mission	Duration of Flight
August 30, 1984	Hartsfield Coats Resnik Hawley Mullane Walker	U.S.A.	STS 41-D (Discovery)	144 hours, 57 minutes

(Walker is the first astronaut from private industry to join a U.S. spaceflight)

Date	Crew	Country	Mission	Duration of Flight
October 5, 1984	Crippen McBride Ride Sullivan Leestma Garneau Scully-Power	U.S.A.	STS 41-G (Challenger)	197 hours, 24 minutes

(Sullivan is first American woman to walk in space)

Date	Crew	Country	Mission	Duration of Flight
November 27, 1985	Shaw O'Connor Cleave Ross Spring Vela Walker	U.S.A.	STS 61-B (Atlantis)	165 hours, 4 minutes

(first structure assembled during spacewalk)

Date	Crew	Country	Mission	Duration of Flight
March 13, 1986	Kizin Soloyvov	U.S.S.R.	Soyuz T-15	3006 hours, 25 minutes

(space station Mir first occupied)

The history of spaceflight has not been one of uninterrupted success. As in the development of other forms of transportation, delays, cancellations, and accidents have happened. The explosion of the Space Shuttle Challenger in 1986, in which all seven astronauts were killed, was the worst accident, but there have been others. In 1967, a Soviet cosmonaut was killed when a parachute failed to open during reentry. In 1971, three other Soviet cosmonauts were killed when the cabin of their spacecraft depressurized too soon.

Yet astronauts and cosmonauts are actually very safe in their vehicles. Numerous backup systems, safety devices, and design features have been added to spacecraft for protection. Since the first astronauts and cosmonauts were rocketed into space, more have died during training on earth than in space. But these accidents have led to the development of safer training and flying practices.

The risks of exploring space will never go away. Space is a hostile environment for human beings. However, the urge to explore and the desire to expand human knowledge have made the risks acceptable to many people. Future advances in high-tech equipment, support systems, and safety procedures will lessen these risks, but there will always be some danger. If you plan to be an astronaut, this goes with the job.

FURTHER READING

Allen, Joseph P., and Martin, Russell. *Entering Space.* New York: Stewart, Tabori & Chang, 1984.

Behrens, June. *Sally Ride, Astronaut: An American First.* Chicago: Children's Press, 1984.

Collins, Michael. *Carrying the Fire: An Astronaut's Journeys.* New York: Farrar, Straus & Giroux, 1974.

Fox, Mary Virginia. *Women Astronauts: Aboard the Shuttle.* New York: Julian Messner/Simon & Schuster, 1985.

Haskins, James, and Benson, Kathleen. *Space Challenger, The Story of Guion Bluford.* Minneapolis: Carolrhoda Books, 1984.

Ride, Sally, with Susan Okie. *To Space and Back.* New York: Lothrop, Lee & Shepard Books, 1986.

Wolfe, Tom. *The Right Stuff.* New York: Farrar, Straus & Giroux, 1979.

3
From Now to the Future

Space travel of the future will depend on rockets and shuttle-type transportation. Both of these systems have their advantages. Despite the success of the space shuttles, rockets will still be necessary in the future.

On July 15, 1975, three U.S. astronauts were boosted into orbit in an Apollo capsule, propelled by a Saturn 1B rocket. This was the last time that U.S. astronauts flew into space using an expendable rocket system, that is, a system that could be used only once. This system was replaced by the reusable space shuttle, which could carry more astronauts, plus cargo, over and over again. Since the first shuttle was launched on April 12, 1981, all U.S. astronauts have traveled into space on board these modern space transports.

The Soviet Union continues to use a rocket system to carry its cosmonauts into orbit, but Soviet engineers have designed and built their own shuttle system based on the American shuttle. The Soviet shuttle is expected to take over personnel launch tasks in the future, but a rocket system will be retained for use in case of delays or breakdowns. Also, unpiloted rockets will be useful in resupplying Soviet space stations and launching satellites.

The U.S. dependence on the shuttle for transporting astronauts and space payloads led to a complete halt in the American space program after the Challenger disaster. Not only was the astronaut program put on hold, but no satellites or scientific experiments could be launched because no working rockets were available.

Now, the U.S. has redeveloped a rocket launching system, based on the reliable Titan boosters originally designed for the Apollo program. The next generation of U.S. rockets is being built by the Martin Marietta Corporation and McDonnell Douglas Astronautics Company. The current Titan rockets can carry no more than 40,000 pounds; with the new rockets, called the Advanced Lift System, satellites as large as 150,000 pounds can be lifted into orbit.

Rockets in the future will make up an unpiloted transportation system for satellites, space station components, and supplies. If necessary, astronauts could be launched along with living quarters or space stations, but the shuttle system is expected to be the primary means of transportation until the next space transportation system—the spaceplane—is developed.

The Space Shuttle

The space shuttle system was developed to provide a reusable launch system that could outperform rockets. This system depends on the most complex vehicle ever created. It took many years and thousands of people to design, test, and manufacture this aircraft. The decision to make a reusable space transportation vehicle has propelled the world from the first stage of space exploration into the future.

The shuttle design came from the Air Force's rocket planes, the X-15 and the X-20. The X-20 was nicknamed "Dyna-Soar," and was designed to be launched into space on top of a rocket, then glide back through the atmosphere, just like the shuttle. The Dyna-Soar was scheduled to be ready for its first flight in 1966, but the project was canceled in 1963, two years after American astronauts had flown into space in the first Mercury launch.

In 1969, the same year that the first astronauts landed on the moon, NASA began designing the Space Shuttle Transportation System (STS). The design was completed in 1972, and Rockwell International was chosen to build the vehicles. The actual spacecraft was called the Orbiting Vehicle (OV), and it would be propelled into space by two reusable solid rocket boosters and an expendable external fuel tank.

Five shuttles were originally built. The first (OV-101) was named Enterprise and never flew into space. It was used for testing, and flew only on the back of a specially modified Boeing 747 and in landing tests. The other four shuttles are: Challenger (OV-099), Columbia (OV-102), Discovery (OV-103), and Atlantis (OV-104). NASA is also constructing a sixth shuttle to replace the Challenger, which was destroyed in the explosion after its launch on January 28, 1986.

Each OV is 37 meters long by 17 meters high. The wingspan is 24 meters. When empty, the vehicle's weight is 75,000 kilograms, or 82.5 tons. The carrying capacity of an OV is 29,500 kilograms, or 32.5 tons, and a crew of seven. On-board life support systems will allow a shuttle to remain in orbit for up to thirty days, but most missions are only a few days in length.

One of the biggest technological breakthroughs that made the shuttle design possible was the development of new heat-protection materials. On the first few vehicles, the nosecap and leading edges of the wings (edges on the front) are made of reinforced carbon-carbon, which can protect against temperatures of up to 1,650 degrees C. Special tiles called high-temperature reusable surface insulation protect against temperatures from 650 degrees C to 1,275 degrees C. Other tiles called low-temperature reusable surface insulation protect against temperatures from 370 degrees C to 650 degrees C. All of these tiles are made from silica that has been fired like ceramics, then painted with a reflective coating. All shuttle surfaces that do not need the advanced protection of these tiles are covered with a special material made of Nomex felt.

On the shuttles built most recently, Discovery and Atlantis, even more advanced materials have been used to replace the silica tiles. Continuing research and development will lead to the next type of protective material that will be used on the spaceplane.

Meanwhile, in other countries, spacecraft similar to the space shuttle are being developed. The Japanese plan to use their expendable rockets, the H-2 models, until a reusable system is ready. The Chinese have a reliable system of launching satellites into orbit using a variety of rockets. With these rockets and a reusable space shuttle vehicle, they will probably begin putting their astronauts into orbit in the near future. The European Space Agency is also working on a mini-space shuttle, called the Hermes. The Hermes will be boosted into orbit using the proven Ariane rocket system.

The space shuttle is an effective aircraft for what it does, but it isn't perfect. It is very expensive to carry each pound of payload—human or cargo—into orbit. Half of the cost of each flight goes into the solid rocket boosters and the external fuel tank. Moreover, between flights, each shuttle must undergo expensive and time-consuming refitting procedures before it is ready to fly again. At best, a shuttle can fly only once a month, carrying at most 27,000 kilograms (30 tons) of cargo into orbit. The shuttle was designed with the best technology available in the 1970s, but major advances have been made since then. For example, new computers are now much smaller, faster, and more powerful. Engine designs have also been improved, using less fuel to produce more thrust. In addition, new construction materials are lighter and stronger, and aerodynamic engineering has advanced, allowing for more efficient aircraft shapes.

In the next phase of space development, the construction of a space station, lunar base, and resupply for space habitations, shuttles and rockets together won't be able to keep up with the demands for transportation. The solution lies in the next generation of space transportation vehicle—the spaceplane.

Spaceplanes will be people carriers for destinations in low earth orbits (up to 250 miles in altitude or 400 kilometers). They will be able to carry more people and cargo and fly more missions than the space shuttles. The United States and the Soviet Union are planning to use spaceplanes for their future space programs, and several other countries have spaceplanes under development.

The United States is developing a spaceplane that will be capable of carrying either cargo or people. It is referred to as a transatmospheric vehicle (TAV), a hypersonic transport, a spaceplane, or the "Orient Express." If used as a long-range transport, it could carry up to five hundred passengers from Seattle to Tokyo in two hours. It would also be useful as a spy plane, flying in orbital missions for surveillance, or it could carry satellites or astronauts into orbit. The key to the TAV design is the special scramjet engines. They will propel the plane off the ground using a mixture of fuel and oxygen from the atmosphere, then convert into ramjets—engines that provide their own oxygen—when the oxygen in the upper atmosphere thins out. During a final stage, they will need rocket power to leave the atmosphere and enter space.

The Next Step in Space

The space shuttle program is really just a delivery service. The shuttles and the astronauts aboard them are mostly carrying satellites into orbit around the earth. In some ways, the shuttle is a space truck. The next step in space development for the United States will be the construction of a space station, similar to the one the Soviet Union has already built.

The space station will be a halfway step for most of the future jobs that will be performed in space. Scientists on board this orbiting laboratory will study many of the problems that future astronauts will face, including the effects of weightlessness and living in cramped quarters for long periods of time and the production of energy and food.

In this artist's conception of the future in space astronauts work on a space station. MCDONNELL DOUGLAS ASTRONAUTICS COMPANY

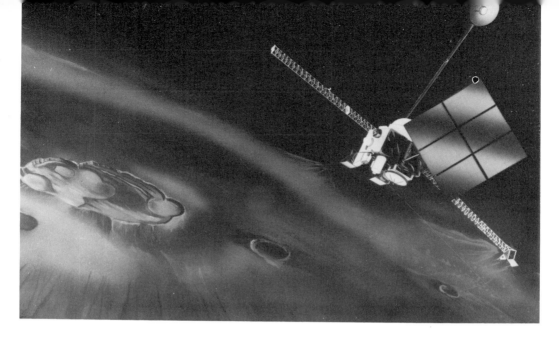

This Mars Observer spacecraft will gather and transmit information about Mars. GENERAL ELECTRIC

The space station will make possible the next stage in the exploration of space—the construction of a lunar base and the first piloted expedition to Mars. Building and living on the lunar base could be easier for astronauts than building and living in the space station, because the low gravity of the moon is less difficult to work in than no gravity at all. For fun and exercise, people on the moon could fly with winglike attachments on their arms.

On the lunar base, some astronauts will perform scientific experiments, from studies of the geology of the moon to astronomical observations from a moon-based space telescope. Other astronauts will operate the life-support systems of the base, recycle the air and water, and grow food. Some astronauts will run robots that will mine minerals from the moon and turn them into useful metals. Others will build spacecraft for exploring the planets in the solar system. One important product that can be made from lunar materials is rocket fuel for trips to the planets.

Before the first astronauts land on Mars, several nonpiloted missions will have already landed and transmitted information to earth about the atmosphere, soil, and conditions on the surface. There is a limit, however, to what even the most advanced devices can discover about strange, new places. In order to fully understand what Mars is like, explorer astronauts will have to go there and see for themselves. Because of the cost of designing and building the vehicle necessary to carry them there, a joint mission may be carried out with the Soviet Union. To many scientists, the Mars mission is the most important and exciting challenge of the future.

Other important developments in space will be:

- building and operating an orbiting spaceport to transfer people and materials to spacecraft headed to the moon base and other space stations;
- operating space "buses" between the orbiting spaceport, other space stations, and the moon base;

Artist's conception of a Teleoperator Maneuvering System, or space tractor, which would be used to move large objects in space, such as these beams for an earth-orbiting platform structure
NASA

- building space platforms for orbiting laboratories, telescopes, and factories. These platforms would be run automatically or by remote control, with astronauts occasionally visiting to repair or replace equipment;
- building space tugs to carry equipment and satellites from one place to another. The space shuttle or the spaceplane can carry astronauts or satellites into a low earth orbit. Low earth orbit is fine for some types of space activity, but many kinds of satellites must be in a higher earth orbit in order to work properly.

Much additional fuel would be required for the shuttle or spaceplane to boost from low earth orbit to high earth orbit. In order to carry this extra fuel, the vehicles must be designed differently, and would have to limit their regular cargoes. Instead, a better vehicle for moving from one orbit to another is a reusable orbital transfer vehicle (ROTV), or space tug. Another kind of space tug is the orbital maneuvering vehicle (OMV), which would operate only in low earth orbit.

The OMV could tow satellites back for repair or return to earth. It could also move satellites into position for orbiting. The ROTV would have a longer range than the OMV, and could move satellites a greater distance. These vehicles would be like tow trucks in space, but they wouldn't need pilots. Instead, computer programs, video cameras, and remote control would allow astronauts to operate the space tugs from the convenience of the space shuttle or space station.

FURTHER READING

Bova, Ben. *Welcome to Moonbase.* New York: Ballantine Books, 1987.

Brand, Stewart, ed. *Space Colonies.* New York: Penguin Books, 1977.

Maurer, Richard. *The NOVA Space Explorer's Guide: Where to Go & What to See.* New York: Clarkson N. Potter, 1985.

National Commission on Space. *Pioneering the Space Frontier: The Report of The National Commission on Space.* New York: Bantam Books, 1986.

O'Leary, Brian. *Mars Nineteen Ninety-Nine: Exclusive Preview of the U.S.–Soviet Manned Mission.* Harrisburg, Pa.: Stackpole Books, 1987.

Stine, Harry G. *Handbook for Space Colonists.* New York: Owl/Holt, 1985.

4
Astronaut Training

Nobody knew exactly what to expect when the first astronauts were chosen to go into space. These astronauts were picked very carefully for their excellent physical condition, ability to work under unknown conditions and stress, and their past experience in piloting aircraft.

Many of the tests for selecting astronauts are no longer used. Although an astronaut-candidate must still be in good physical and mental condition, extreme physical tests have proven to be unnecessary.

The first astronauts were chosen only from candidates who were test pilots. The experience of being a test pilot was thought to be a good measure for conditioning, working under stress, and reacting quickly to new situations. Test pilots were also familiar with technical and engineering work, so they could be valuable in understanding and helping to modify the then new space vehicles.

NASA still requires candidates for the positions of astronaut pilot and commander to have flying experience. Mission specialists and payload specialists do not have to be pilots. As space exploration becomes more sophisticated, the astronaut's role will grow more specialized. Even now, a shuttle mission will include the following special kinds of astronauts:

Astronaut pilot. The astronaut who actually flies the shuttle. Most shuttle missions have an experienced astronaut pilot and a rookie pilot on board.

Mission specialist. An astronaut who is trained to carry out scientific experiments. Most mission specialists are expected to fly on twenty to thirty shuttle missions.

Payload specialist. An astronaut who is trained to carry out specific tasks or scientific experiments on a special flight. Because the payload specialist has specialized training only for certain flights, he or she may only fly on a few shuttle missions. Most payload specialists are already experts in a particular scientific area before they go through a short astronaut-training course to prepare for a mission. Since they do not have to learn how to fly the shuttle or operate its systems (except for the life-support systems such as the zero-gravity toilet), their astronaut training may last only a few months.

Manned spaceflight engineers (MSE). An astronaut who is also a military officer, trained to participate in the design, testing, and deployment of military payloads. MSEs do not apply to NASA for this job but are picked by a special group of military personnel according to their qualifications. Like other astronauts, MSEs have studied different sciences in college, and most have more than one college degree. Unlike the other military astronauts, MSEs do not have to be pilots.

Civilian astronaut. A passenger on board a shuttle mission who has gone through the minimum training program from NASA. Usually, this person is part of a private, nongovernment project that is trying to develop profitable manufacturing techniques in zero-gravity.

Physical Condition

An astronaut candidate has to be in good physical condition. Medical problems could make a space mission ineffective and even dangerous. Medical tests of candidates identify those physiological problems that are considered unsuitable for astronauts. Such problems as hearing loss, defective vision, asthma, heart murmurs or irregularities, liver malfunctions, ulcers, and life-threatening diseases can prevent a candidate from becoming an astronaut. It is not necessary, however, to have perfect hearing or vision to be acceptable.

Many of the dangers that were anticipated for humans in space turned out not to be problems after all. The G-forces (see Glossary) that the rocket boosters created were minor compared to what pilots were used to experiencing. Spacesickness, also called space adaptation syndrome (SAS), has created the most problems, but these are not serious.

So far, NASA has been unable to devise a test that can predict who will suffer from spacesickness. Flying in the special KC-135 plane, also known as the "vomit comet," produces periods of weightlessness for as long as thirty seconds. This experience makes many people sick, but some of them do not have the same reaction in the weightlessness of space itself. Some people who got sick on the KC-135 did not suffer from spacesickness in orbit, but other people who did not get sick on the KC-135 did. In most cases, however, spacesickness goes away in a few days.

Many astronauts who were not chosen after taking NASA's tests the first time applied again and were accepted. Sometimes this was because they learned more when they went back to college or worked on scientific projects. NASA also changes its tests and requirements

Astronauts endure training in the KC-135, the "vomit comet," which produces brief periods of weightlessness that can cause spacesickness.
NASA

Astronauts evaluate the handrail system during a long extra-vehicular activity (EVA) aboard the Challenger. NASA

from time to time, and something that keeps a candidate from passing the first time may no longer be a problem the second time around.

Floating around inside a space shuttle in zero-gravity does not require much effort. In fact, almost everything that is done in space requires little effort, yet astronauts must be in very good physical shape. Why? Because being in good shape helps prevent sickness, makes people more alert, and allows the body to stay busier for longer periods without tiring. One aspect of space travel that does require a great deal of endurance is extravehicular activity (EVA)—spacewalking. Astronauts who have experienced EVA have described it as very physically tiring.

Almost all astronaut candidates have participated in sports and exercise activities. These include swimming, skiing, jogging, basketball, football, baseball, racquetball, scuba diving, and bicycling. What is important is regular exercise that builds cardiovascular conditioning and develops coordination. What is not important is being a weight-lifting champion or being the fastest runner on the track team.

Psychological Condition

An astronaut must not have an unstable mental condition that could endanger a mission or the lives of a crew. Nor can an astronaut have trouble working with other people, because the success of a mission depends upon the mutual cooperation of its members. NASA looks for astronaut candidates who are well-balanced people who get along with others and can adapt to the sometimes stressful conditions of space travel.

Astronaut candidates are interviewed by psychologists and psychiatrists during the testing program. They also take written tests. Although this type of testing seems relatively simple, cheating is not possible, because the interviews and the tests don't have right and wrong answers. The goal is to weed out those who may not react quickly and safely in emergencies or during dull, routine work in the hostile environment of space.

Since NASA began testing candidates for the astronaut program, very few have been turned down because of psychological concerns. About the only problem that has kept candidates from being accepted is claustrophobia, the fear of enclosed spaces.

Pilot Training

It is no longer necessary for all astronauts to be pilots. Some candidates might be sent to flight school after selection if they do not already have piloting experience. Flight training has proven to be effective in preparing space shuttle passengers for the sensations of riding in a vehicle that is maneuvered into many unusual positions.

In the past, NASA gave preference to scientists who had valuable skills if they were also pilots. This situation is changing, however, as the space program becomes more complex and more people are needed to carry out new assignments. For instance, the simulator for the MMU (see Glossary) is a complex machine that requires dexterity and good hand-eye coordination. But experienced pilots who have good dexterity and coordination usually take longer to get the hang of this device than nonfliers.

The U.S. astronaut corps uses the space shuttle as its only form of transportation to space and back. Because something could go wrong during the launch or reentry phase of a mission, the space shuttle might not be able to land at its designated spot. A forced landing at sea or in a remote area makes survival training a necessity for all astronauts.

This training involves demonstrations and practice. Emergency exits from shuttle mock-ups are practiced on dry land and in the water. Methods of using rafts and helicopter retrievals are part of this program. Astronauts who take flight instruction must also learn ejection techniques and the use of parachutes.

Astronaut candidate Shannon W. Lucid practices emergency sea landings as part of an intensive survival training program. NASA

Classroom Training Most of the astronaut's time during the first year is spent in classrooms, learning new material. Astronauts must learn how the shuttle is constructed, how it works, and how to operate the life-support systems, as well as the complex flight controls and many console monitors, equipment controls, and computers. They must also study ground-control operations.

Astronauts must be familiar with every aspect of the system that runs each spaceflight. Even though astronauts have already become experts in specialized fields before being accepted into the space program, they must also learn about other subjects. In space, astronauts have to do many things, and understanding different sciences and procedures ensures that they will be able to do the job.

Technical Training After a year of classroom study, astronauts begin several years of specialized assignments, in which they work alongside scientists, technicians, and engineers who are putting together the shuttle system. This work is necessary as the shuttles are constantly being upgraded, modified, and studied to improve their performance.

Other assignments include learning about mission control, testing new procedures in the KC-135 plane, and advanced pilot training. Shuttle pilots must become familiar with the complex controls of this high-tech spacecraft. Many different simulators are used to duplicate the effects of flying the shuttle. These include a shuttle training aircraft, navigation simulator, systems engineering simulator, shuttle mission simulator, and motion-base simulator.

Some special assignments for astronauts involve working for companies that NASA has paid to design shuttle equipment. Astronauts provide valuable information, because they are the ones who will be using this equipment. Satellites or other shuttle payloads may also require special astronaut assignments.

Mission control always uses an astronaut during missions to relay voice communications to the orbiting crew. This astronaut has completed the same training as the crew and can therefore respond more quickly if a problem develops. Working at mission control also gives astronauts more information about how the ground-support system helps the crew during a mission.

Astronauts who will be wearing spacesuits and space walking must

Astronauts train in the Johnson Space Center's weightless environment test facility. NASA

have advanced training. Much of this is accomplished in a large swimming pool called a weightless environment training facility. An astronaut wearing a spacesuit in this tank is not completely weightless, but being in the tank feels almost like being in space.

Other advanced training is done with the remote manipulator arm simulator and the manned maneuvering unit simulator. These gadgets can be fun, but most of the work that astronauts do to prepare for missions is less exciting and more tedious. Astronauts must have good study skills and be motivated enough to stay attentive during their training.

Future Training Astronauts today can only fly missions that use the space shuttle. In the future, space stations, other space vehicles, and bases on the moon and other planets will require a different kind of astronaut and different kinds of training.

Spacecraft pilots will need the most specialized training. But because fewer activities in space will be carried out on board the transport vehicle, the pilots will have less involvement with other space operations and will spend less time in orbit. Their jobs will resemble those of airline pilots, delivering and returning people and payloads from orbit.

Astronaut Henry W. Hartsfield, Jr., demonstrates the sleeping accommodations aboard the Columbia. NASA

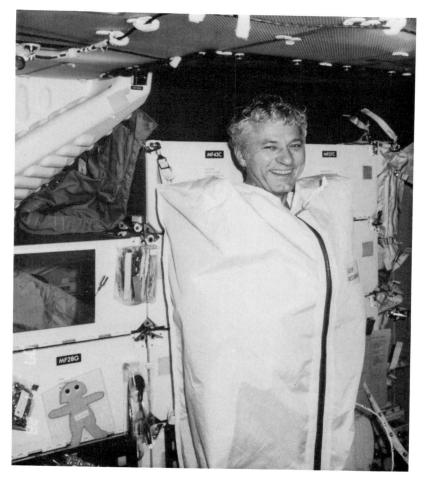

In the future, astronauts who remain in space for longer periods aboard the space station or other spacecraft will need less training than today's astronauts. Their jobs will require more in-depth scientific and engineering skills, not detailed knowledge of the operating systems of the vehicle they live on.

These space workers will spend most of their time doing work in their specialized fields. As scientists, they must be good at what they do, but they will also have to know a little about living in space. Their preflight training will take only a few weeks or months, just long enough to familiarize them with the life-support systems, emergency procedures, and exercise programs necessary for zero-gravity conditions.

The space station and other space habitations will include some crew members with advanced knowledge about the systems and operations. These astronauts must be able to monitor, adjust, and repair equipment that isn't working properly. There must also be someone in charge. This person will be the most knowledgeable about the space structure and will have the training and leadership abilities to command its crew.

O'Leary, Brian. *The Making of an Ex-Astronaut.* Boston: Houghton Mifflin, 1970. **FURTHER READING**

5
Jobs in Space

A Shuttle Mission The crew of a space shuttle can range from two to seven in number. During takeoff, reentry, and landing, the crew rides in the forward cabin of the shuttle. The shuttle commander is in charge of the mission, and is responsible for ensuring the safety of the crew, managing the flight, and overseeing the tasks that are scheduled to be performed by the crew. The commander's seat is on the left of the forward flight deck, facing the instrument panel. The commander usually flies the shuttle.

The shuttle pilot is also trained to fly the shuttle. He or the shuttle commander can take over if any problems arise with the computerized flight sequences. When the shuttle ends its reentry phase and approaches the landing strip, the pilot or commander takes over from the computer just before landing. The pilot's seat is on the right of the forward flight deck, facing the instrument panel.

One astronaut mission specialist also sits on the forward flight deck. This seat is located on the right side, just behind the pilot's seat. Next to it is a seat for an astronaut payload specialist or scientist.

The other members of the crew sit in the mid-deck section. All of the seats except for the commander's and the pilot's are unfastened and stored after the shuttle reaches orbit. Because the shuttle is operating in micro-gravity conditions, there is no need for the crew to sit "down."

Once the shuttle has reached its predetermined altitude, the commander or pilot can change its position with the orbital maneuvering system (OMS) or reaction control system (RCS). These systems are necessary for adjusting the direction of the vehicle or moving it from one orbit to another.

During the orbiting phase of a shuttle flight, the crew works at the aft crew station, which is located at the back of the forward flight deck, behind the commander's and pilot's seats. This station is equipped with instrument consoles and controls that allow the crew to maneuver, monitor payloads, and operate the remote manipulator system (RMS).

Astronauts Jeffrey Hoffman and S. David Griggs work together on the remote manipulator system arm of the Discovery. NASA

Astronaut Bruce Mc-Candless II moves through space using the manned maneuvering unit (MMU), a backpack power device. NASA

The astronaut mission specialist has a working position on the left of the aft crew station, facing the rear. The payload specialist has a working position on the right side. Both specialists have monitors, computers, and controls to carry out their assigned jobs.

The pilot and payload handler have work stations between the left and right work positions on the aft crew station. The shuttle maneuvering controls that the pilot uses are on the left, and the controls for the maneuvering arm and the video monitor that the payload handler uses are on the right.

During a typical shuttle mission, the crew is responsible for launching satellites from the payload bay. Sometimes it is necessary to retrieve satellites that are already in orbit. This may require extra-vehicular activity (EVA), which means that one or two crew members will have to put on a spacesuit, or extravehicular mobility unit (EMU), and take a space walk. If necessary, an astronaut may have to use the manned maneuvering unit (MMU) during EVA to move from the shuttle to another spacecraft or satellite.

Some shuttle flights carry spacelabs, which are enclosed modules in the payload bay for conducting scientific experiments. The modules are connected to the shuttle mid-deck by a tunnel. Scientists and engineers who are not full-time astronauts may be part of a shuttle mission in order to work on experiments in the spacelab. Even if they fly on only one mission, these professionals must go through astronaut training in order to be prepared for flying and living on the shuttle.

At the end of a mission, the shuttle crew must prepare for leaving orbit by cleaning the crew quarters, storing equipment, closing the payload doors, and refastening the crew seats. The commander or pilot begins reentry by maneuvering the shuttle into proper position for the de-orbit engine burn. Following the de-orbit burn, additional maneuvering positions the shuttle to protect it during the intense heat buildup of reentry into the atmosphere. Beginning at 6,000 meters, the shuttle is piloted through a series of "S" turn maneuvers that slow its descent through the atmosphere. At 600 meters, the controls are used to roll and bank the vehicle for final slowing. At 27 meters above the ground—only 14 seconds before touchdown—the landing gear is lowered, and the shuttle makes its final approach and landing.

Following every flight, the shuttle crew works with ground-control specialists during debriefing. This important task allows NASA to analyze the performance of the spacecraft, the efficiency of the work schedule, and the effectiveness of the mission. Astronauts are also examined by doctors to check their response to micro-gravity conditions and return to normal gravity. Mission specialists and payload specialists may also work with satellite companies to analyze the launching and performance of the equipment.

LAUNCH SATELLITES

The space shuttle was designed to launch satellites, and much of the work that astronauts do on these spacecraft involves deploying satellites. Most of these satellites, and those launched by rockets in the United States and around the world, are communications satellites. Even though there are already hundreds of these satellites in orbit around the earth, thousands more will be launched in the future.

Advances in technology will produce more efficient communications satellites, and new regulations will allow twice as many in the same area as before. Because there are so many practical uses for

What Will Astronauts of the Future Do in Space?

A payload assist module (PAM), carrying two communications satellites, eases out of the cargo bay of the Challenger. MCDONNELL DOUGLAS ASTRONAUTICS COMPANY

these devices, and many different companies eager to use them, they will continue to increase.

Astronauts on future shuttles and spaceplanes will compete with unpiloted rocket launching systems to carry satellites into orbit. The astronaut mission specialists and payload specialists can expect most of their work to be routine, just as it has been in the past. However, astronauts can react if something goes wrong during a satellite deployment, which cannot be done on rocket-boosted satellites. They will use the RMA or go for a space walk, if necessary, to repair equipment or retrieve broken satellites for return to earth.

Satellite repair will also become a major activity on the space station. Space tugs can be sent on missions to adjust or repair the satellites, using remote-control devices. Astronauts will direct this activity with the aid of video monitors to see what is going on.

Communications satellites are usually placed in orbit in a narrow band of space above the earth's equator. At a distance of about 36,000 kilometers above the earth, these satellites are in geostationary orbits (GEO), so-called because they move at the same speed as the earth and therefore remain at the same spot in the sky relative to the earth. Occasional drifting in orbit can cause these satellites to move from their assigned positions. Special, small rockets are used to adjust a satellite's position if it has strayed.

One problem with GEO satellites is that they are bombarded with radiation and particles from space, which can cause malfunctions of on-board computers and electronics. Satellites can also run out of propellant for their rockets.

A future job for astronauts will be operating a space station or satellite repair platform near the ring of GEO satellites. Specialists in electronics, communications technology, and electrical engineering will test and fix satellites and upgrade old components. These astronauts may work only on specific satellites for the companies that made them or they may be trained to work on any type that needs fixing.

FLY MILITARY MISSIONS

Most of the advances in space exploration have come from the military. Rockets were first developed to carry explosives over long distances. The race between the Soviets and the Americans to take advantage of the "high ground" of space has fueled the drive to put people into space. Astronauts and satellites in orbit can spy on the other side and communicate more effectively with their own earth-based forces.

In the future, military uses of space will depend upon the political relationships between the countries that have space transportation systems. The "Star Wars" system that the U.S. is developing, which will use satellite weapons to destroy enemy missiles, will create many new jobs in the future, even if it is only partly built. Jobs for astronauts in the future will also come from military budgets, even if no weapons are involved. Advances in surveillance and communications technology will create many of these jobs.

MANUFACTURE MATERIALS

The communications satellite business is estimated to be worth billions of dollars. Space manufacturing is going to be even bigger. Most of the success will come from using micro-gravity to produce new kinds of materials that can't be made on earth.

The NASA term for space manufacturing is materials processing in space (MPS). The science of research into the behavior of materials in the absence of gravity is called micro-gravity science and applications.

Gravity is not completely absent in orbiting vehicles. When in orbit, objects are falling forward, around the curvature of the earth. The momentum created by this forward motion cancels the effect of earth's gravity, which should be pulling objects down toward the center of the planet. People and things in orbit are all falling forward at the same rate of speed, and so have the same lack of "weight" relative to each other. A toothbrush and an astronaut both weigh the same in this condition. There is still a very small effect from gravitational attraction—about one-millionth of the earth's gravity—but it is too small to notice in most situations. Scientists usually refer to the gravitational environment of orbit as micro-gravity.

Products that have already been studied in space for possible improvement back on earth include arc lights, cast iron, semiconductor crystals, and pharmaceutical drugs. These products are made from materials that can be improved through space research and manufacturing.

Crystals and alloys. Electronic devices depend on microchips for their computing power. New types of high-efficiency microchips could be made from semiconductor crystals grown in spacelabs, because these crystals would not suffer the damaging effects of gravity. Alloys of some materials are difficult or impossible to make on earth because gravity separates the components. In space, the lack of gravity allows mixtures of many different materials. Some of these combinations could create stronger, lighter metals.

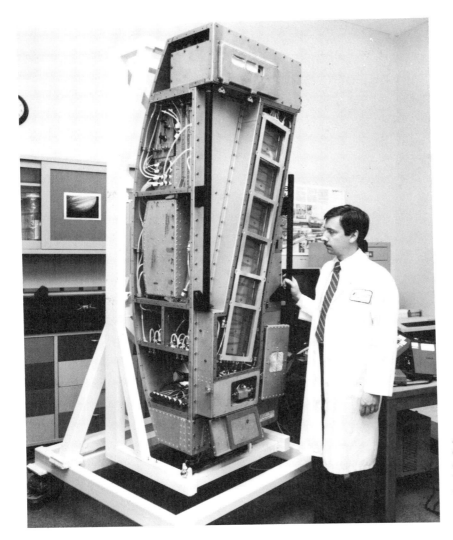

An electrophoresis device for sorting compounds in space to produce pharmaceuticals MCDONNELL DOUGLAS ASTRONAUTICS COMPANY

Containerless processing. Products made on earth can never be completely pure, because they are contaminated by whatever they touch. Unwanted substances can be added to the final material, or the container or mold creates an imperfect shape. Containers would not be needed in space because the lack of gravity would keep materials from spreading out. Some geometric shapes, such as perfect mirrors for reflecting telescopes, could also be cast without a mold.

Biological materials processing. Drugs that can help humans live longer, healthier lives can be made in space. Micro-gravity processing can be used to increase the purity of drugs and separate complex compounds into usable components. Electrophoresis, a system of sorting compounds using an electrical current, is a highly effective method of doing this in space.

The space transportation systems now available are already capable of boosting into orbit self-contained automated laboratories and small materials-processing systems. However, the cost is at least several thousand dollars per pound. Anything that is produced must then be sold for more dollars per pound in order to make a profit. According to one estimate, a product made in space must be sold for a million dollars a pound to pay back the cost of making it there.

Obviously, there aren't many products that are worth that kind of money. However, in the future, the competition among the space shuttle, spaceplane, and rockets to boost materials into orbit will bring the cost per pound down by as much as seventy-five percent. Then it will be possible to manufacture products that will have more appeal on earth.

The task of researching and creating products in space will be left to special astronauts with engineering and scientific backgrounds. Chemists, biologists, physicists, and other types of scientists will be needed to work in the space-based laboratories. Some of these specialized workers will also be needed on earth.

Many of the technical processes that will be carried out in space can be done by automated equipment. However, some specialists will still need to monitor the equipment, make adjustments, and observe results. There are still no machines that can replace the human eye and brain for certain tasks.

LIVE IN SPACE STATIONS

Soviet cosmonauts have already demonstrated that humans can live for long periods of time in orbiting space stations. Plans for a U.S. space station have been ready for years, and the first American astronauts may soon occupy it. This space station will provide many jobs for astronauts to do.

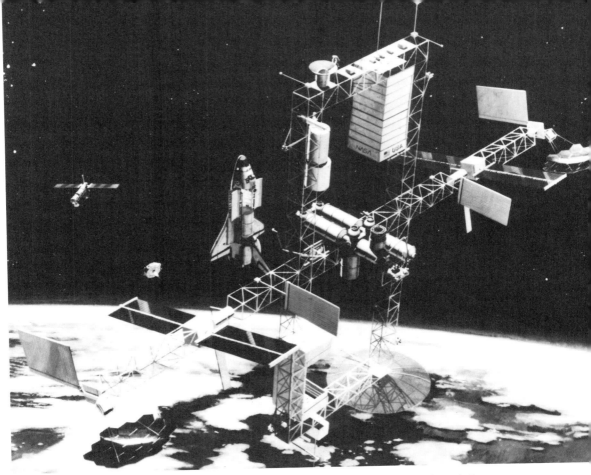

An artist's conception of a space station LOCKHEED MISSILES & SPACE COMPANY, INC.

The space station will be a base for scientific experiments. It will include a high-tech laboratory that can conduct important research into the effects of micro-gravity. Other research efforts will study solar and cosmic radiation, weather patterns on earth, and long-range communications. Doctors will work with astronauts to study the effects of micro-gravity on humans. Psychologists will study the effects of living in cramped conditions away from earth. Biologists will help develop systems to grow vegetables with hydroponics. Engineers will design and modify life-support systems to recycle oxygen and water.

The space station can also be a "bus stop" for astronauts on their way to other destinations. Space shuttles or spaceplanes can drop their passengers at the space station, where they will transfer to relay vehicles for trips to the moon or other planets.

An additional lunar space station would probably be built as part of the lunar base project. This orbiting lunar station would circle the moon about two hundred miles above the surface or be located at one of the Lagrange points (see Glossary). The station would be a relay point for astronauts traveling from the earth to the lunar base, as well as a base for scientific experiments and communications functions.

MINE EXTRATERRESTRIAL MINERALS

A mass driver, designed for mining objects such as ore on the moon. The mass driver would accelerate the ore into space, where it would be stopped by a special net. NASA

Future astronauts will become miners in space. Unlike most miners on earth, they will need special engineering training to operate robot machines that will do the actual work. The moon, planets, and asteroids are rich in minerals that can be used to manufacture space habitats, spacecraft, and fuel. Examination of lunar rocks and soil brought back from the Apollo missions reveal deposits of aluminum, silicon, iron, nickel, and titanium on the moon. Scientists have discovered that concrete made from pulverized lunar rocks is a little stronger than concrete made on earth. This lunar concrete could be

used to construct habitats and buildings for the astronauts living on the moon base.

Oxygen for life-support systems can also be mined from some types of ores. The most sought after "ore" will be plain old water. Deposits of ice could become the gold mines of the future, because the cost of boosting this simple substance from earth into space will make it a rare and critical resource.

The most sought after ores on earth contain gold, silver, and platinum. Some asteroids also have ores that contain these valuable metals. Space miners will prospect for rich asteroid lodes with remote sensors, then use automated extractors to refine the material before shipping it back to earth as return cargo on the space shuttle or spaceplane.

Some ores that will be mined on the moon could also be useful in other locations in space. A special device called a mass driver has already been invented for transporting material such as ore from one area in space to another. The mass driver works by accelerating objects through an electromagnetic field until they reach a speed that will carry them out of a gravitational field. Because there is no friction from air in space, the objects would keep moving until they are stopped by a special net. The mass drivers could be aimed to push ore to processing plants on space stations, spacecraft, or asteroids.

EXPLORE THE UNKNOWN

Astronauts in the future will play an important role in expanding our frontiers, just as explorers on earth discovered unknown jungles, deserts, and lands in the polar regions.

In the future, scientists plan to build a lunar base as a terminal for exploring other planets. The moon has many advantages as an exploration base. Among these are:

- reduced gravity (one-sixth the gravity on earth), allowing for more efficient work and less fuel necessary to reach space;
- large quantities of raw materials that could be used to build housing and spacecraft;
- large quantities of raw materials for making oxygen and fuel for spacecraft.

The first planet that astronauts expect to explore is Mars. Both the United States and Russia have plans to send astronauts to this planet, and are talking of combining both missions into one joint effort. How and when this might occur is still a question, but it is certain that important discoveries are waiting on Mars because of the evidence gathered by astronomers and unpiloted probes already sent there.

Asteroids are also important destinations for future astronauts. Some of them are big enough to provide large quantities of raw materials for fuel and construction of space habitations. Moreover, scientists can learn more about the origin of the solar system by examining these celestial objects.

In the future, many space explorations will be carried out by unpiloted spacecraft. Powerful remote sensing tests and robots can probe distant space objects more inexpensively and efficiently than astronauts can. However, a widespread scientific effort to explore our universe will require building, maintaining, and monitoring these machines from a space station or lunar base. Scientists and engineers will work there to support these missions.

One of the most important kinds of exploration is the advancement of scientific knowledge. Science can sometimes provide benefits for

The Hubble Space Telescope NASA

people by discovering new materials and products, but it is rarely possible to know in advance the outcome of an experiment or observation. Scientists in space will have important jobs to do as they learn more about the universe and the forces and elements of which it is made.

Astronomers using space telescopes will be able to see much farther and in greater detail than they could by using earth-based telescopes, because the lack of atmosphere and light pollution will increase the effectiveness of these scientific tools. Space telescopes in orbit can relay information to astronomers on earth. These telescopes are very sensitive to vibration and actually perform better if there are no humans around. Most space telescopes are operated by astronomers who sit at the computer control panels on earth and use computer programs or tele-operation. These orbiting telescopes eventually fall out of orbit and burn up in the earth's atmosphere.

The Hubble Space Telescope, which will be launched in 1990 or 1991, is an astronomical observatory that will remain in orbit for a very long time. It will be upgraded as new equipment becomes available. Astronauts will deliver and install the new equipment, but the observations will still be done from earth.

Experience gained from using this instrument will allow bigger, more powerful telescopes to be designed for future use on a space platform or lunar base. Materials-processing in space will also help perfect this telescope, because the magnifying mirrors can be enlarged and made with fewer imperfections up in space than under the conditions of gravity on earth.

Bova, Ben. *Welcome to Moonbase*. New York: Ballantine Books, 1987.
Joels, Kerry M., and Kennedy, Gregory P. *The Space Shuttle Operators' Manual*. New York: Ballantine Books, 1982.
Oberg, James E., and Oberg, Alcestis R. *Pioneering Space*. New York: McGraw-Hill, 1986.
Weiss, Malcolm. *Far Out Factories: Manufacturing in Space*. New York: Lodestar Books/E.P. Dutton, 1984.

FURTHER READING

6

Mission 1: Learn!

You can begin preparing for a career in space by making sure that you have a good, well-rounded education by the time you graduate from high school. Classroom learning is the key to becoming good at whatever you do as an adult. You may even decide that you like a special subject or career so much that taking time out to become an astronaut would be a mistake. In any case, you'll never get to make this decision if you don't succeed at this first mission.

These are the areas on which you should concentrate:

Math. You should take mathematics every year during junior and senior high school, including algebra, geometry, and trigonometry. If your school offers the opportunity, calculus is also valuable.

Science. Introductory courses should include physics, chemistry, and biology. If available, also take computer courses and any advanced science courses for which you are eligible.

English. You won't get far in any career without good basic English skills. You may not even get into college. Take English or writing courses every year in junior and senior high school.

Foreign languages. Study at least one foreign language for at least two years in high school. You can also get a head start by taking a language in junior high school, if language courses are available. For science careers, the best languages are German, French, or Russian.

Other subjects. An astronaut, scientist, or engineer must be familiar with many other subjects. You should study history, geography, and social science. Other subjects that are important are sociology, psychology, and economics.

In addition to studying specific subjects, you need to concentrate on developing good study habits. By the time you are ready to train to be an astronaut, homework will not go away, it will get heavier. Good study habits are formed by setting aside a certain time every day to do your schoolwork. You can help yourself by making a schedule and writing down the time you spend studying.

Part of a good education is learning how to find information. The best place to find information is the library. You can use the library at your school, or go to a public or university library. Librarians are there to help; they can introduce you to the special sources that are kept there, or help you find an answer to a specific question.

Other sources of information that you may have at home are encyclopedias, science books, magazines, and a personal computer. With your personal computer, you can dial up electronic information sources that have on-line encyclopedias, indexes of magazine articles, and statistics on many different subjects. You must become a member of these electronic information clubs if you want to use them, and they are not free. If you do use on-line services, make sure you have permission from your parents or school before you begin. For more information about using your computer, see chapter 7.

Summer Studies

Summer camps provide a great way to advance your learning about favorite subjects. Many summer camps across the country now have science and computer classes. If you or your parents are looking at choices for summer camp, you can find out ahead of time if they will offer such courses.

Some camps specialize in certain subjects. There are special summer camps for computers, astronomy, biology, ecology, general science, and foreign languages. These camps are not just for study, however. They also offer recreation and fun, from swimming to horseback riding, depending on the camp.

If you are interested in one of these special camps, the following publication lists their locations, costs, and age limits for campers: *Parents' Guide to Accredited Camps: The Official American Camping Association Guide.* Check your local library or bookstore or order from:

American Camping Association
5000 State Road 67 North
Martinsville, IN 46151
1-800-428-2267 (outside Indiana)
317-342-8456 (inside Indiana)

Science Fairs   Science fairs were first held at a few schools in the United States in the 1920s. Since then, they have spread to almost every school in the country. Competitions are held at individual schools, among school districts, and at statewide, national, and international levels. Science fairs are an excellent way to learn more about a subject that interests you. Science projects take up extra time after school and on weekends, but they will improve your understanding of important scientific principles and teach you valuable study skills, concentration, and perseverance.

Pick a subject that interests you, one that you would like to know more about. Do not pick something that is completely unknown to you or too difficult for your grade level. The most important goal in science fair projects is not to impress the judges with a complex subject but to carry out a sensible plan of investigation following the scientific method.

The scientific method is a way of using logic to answer a question. There are no rules to this method, but these steps are usually followed:

- observation (taking notice of something interesting)
- hypothesis (making a guess about what the observation means)
- test (experimenting to find out whether your guess is right)
- conclusion (what did the experiment prove?)

Future astronauts are often interested in science projects about rockets or astronomy. You can use model rockets or telescopes that you may already have to study scientific principles, such as propul-

Using a reflecting
telescope and a
piece of cardboard,
a future astronaut
demonstrates a safe
way to view the sun.
CATHIE HAVENS,
S&S OPTIKA, DENVER,
COLORADO

sion, gravity, or planetary orbits. There are many other subjects that
relate to space exploration that you can study. Examples are:

- robotics and remote control systems
- computer programs
- ecosystems
- comparative biology
- nutrition
- geology
- optical illusions
- sensory deprivation

Science Contests   Your school's science fair is not the only kind of science contest. Many other science contests are held, which offer local, regional, and national levels of competition. If your teacher or counselor isn't familiar with any of the following, he or she can write for more information.

National Science Olympiad Tournament. This is an annual competition with separate groups for sixth through ninth grades and ninth through twelfth grades. Students compete in such events as metric estimation, paper airplane race, science bowl, and an egg drop contest.

National Science Olympiad Tournament
5955 Little Pine Lane
Rochester, MI 48064

The Odyssey of the Mind. This is a contest for students enrolled in gifted student programs. Teams compete in creative solutions to problems. Skills and talents used include art, drama, music, and logic. Students in elementary and middle schools are eligible.

Odyssey of the Mind Association
P.O. Box 27
Glassboro, NJ 08028

Junior Academy of Sciences. This group is sponsored by the American Association for the Advancement of Science. There is an annual competition with two levels: junior level for seventh, eighth, and ninth grades; and senior level, for tenth, eleventh, and twelfth grades. Students, who can enter independently or be sponsored by a teacher, write and submit science reports to the contest. Awards are given for the best entries.

Junior Academy of Sciences/AAAS
1333 H Street NW
Washington, DC 20005

Space Science Student Involvement Program. This contest is sponsored by NASA and the National Science Teachers Association. Students in grades seven through twelve compete by designing experiments that could be carried out on the space station, the Zero Gravity

Research Facility at NASA Lewis Research Center in Cleveland, Ohio, or the wind tunnel at NASA Langley Research Center in Hampton, Virginia. Other parts of the contest include writing articles for school newspapers and illustrating designs for space colonies. Winners attend a national Space Symposium, visit space research facilities, or receive college scholarships.

SSSIP
National Science Teachers Association
1742 Connecticut Avenue NW
Washington, D.C. 20009

Duracell Scholarship Competition. Students in grades nine through twelve compete by designing and building working devices that use one or more Duracell batteries. Winners receive college scholarships.

Duracell, Inc.
National Science Teachers Association
1742 Connecticut Avenue NW
Washington, D.C. 20009

Mathematics Competition. This contest offers six levels of competition for students in grades six through twelve. There are five contests—each one similar to a math test—held every school year, and scores from each contest are added together. A final national ranking is figured for all of the schools that participate, and plaques and ribbons are awarded for the best individual and school scores.

National Mathematics League
P.O. Box 9459
Coral Springs, FL 33075

Science Competition. This contest—much like a science test—is similar to the Mathematics Competition, with six levels of competition for students in grades six through twelve. Awards are based on the scores from five different contests.

National Science League, Inc.
P.O. Box 9700
Coral Springs, FL 33075

MATHCOUNTS. If you have ever been in a spelling bee, you will understand how this competition works. Students in the seventh and eighth grades are eligible and study with teachers to prepare themselves for contests against students from other schools. Trophies, ribbons, or scholarships are awarded, and winners of city-wide contests get free trips to the state contests, in which they compete in individual and team events. State winners get free trips to Washington for the national contest. MATHCOUNTS is also sponsored by NASA, which gives the national winners free trips to shuttle launches or Space Camp.

MATHCOUNTS
National Society of Professional Engineers
1420 King Street
Alexandria, VA 22314

The National Science Test. This competition doesn't have any prizes, but it provides a challenge by furnishing test scores from around the country for comparison. The National Science Test was originally broadcast on the "NOVA" science show on PBS. You can take the test by reading the book, which has all the original questions: *The Nova National Science Test,* by Ted Bogosian and WGBH Boston, published by New American Library in 1985.

School Clubs   Sometimes the most educational experiences aren't in a classroom. You can enjoy yourself, be with your friends, and study your favorite subjects in special clubs. Most schools help organize and run these groups. Clubs are not like classrooms, where most of the students aren't very interested in the subject. In a club, all of the members share your interests, and you spend more time on the subject. Clubs also sponsor visits from scientists, professionals, and other experts who describe their work and answer questions in detail.

If your school doesn't have a club for the subject that interests you, ask a teacher to help start one. Subjects that might interest future astronauts include astronomy, biology, chemistry, computers, geography, geology, math, pre-med, photography, and physics.

Advanced Study   You may find that math and science courses in your school are boring because you already know the material being taught. Most schools have special programs that will help you find advanced courses in nearby high schools or colleges. If these programs aren't available, your teacher, principal, or guidance counselor may be able to help set up a special independent study course for you.

Poets in Space?

Most people think of astronauts as well-trained professionals who are pilots or engineers. Scientists have also joined the astronaut ranks, and many are now training to work aboard the space shuttle. In the future, there could be room for many other types of people in space. The development of large space stations, space colonies, or bases on the moon or planets will create opportunities for other kinds of experts. Some astronauts have creative talents, but their jobs in space don't allow much time for nonessential tasks. Future astronauts will have more time to spend on relaxation and entertainment. In the future, some of the people in space will be artists, journalists, filmmakers, musicians, playwrights, poets, and clowns. These individuals will be an important part of the new way of life in space because they will find creative ways to express the emotions of those who live in artificial environments far away from this planet. However, these creative people who want to go into space should acquire some scientific understanding.

The Math Monster

Math is usually the most hated subject in school. More kids dislike math than anything else they are taught, and if you ask your parents, chances are that most of them felt the same way when they were your age.

If you are one of these people, you have an important mission to accomplish right now. You are going to have to face up to the "math monster," because if you want to become an astronaut you must be prepared to learn a lot of math. The good news is that there are things you can do to make this mission easier and more enjoyable.

Why do astronauts have to be good at math? Because almost everything that is done in space or in other forms of modern technology is based on how objects and forces act. Everything from gravity to orbits acts in predictable ways if you know the "magic" formulas—and every formula is a form of math.

Many kids, and adults, too, are afraid of math because they think that these "magic" formulas are very complex and impossible for anyone but geniuses to understand. It's true that there are many long and complicated formulas in science, but even the biggest formulas are made up of smaller parts, and many of these smaller parts are as simple as adding and subtracting.

The trick to beating your fear of math is to look for the small parts. Learn the simplest math principles well, and you will be ready for the worst monster equations. Just like hitting a baseball or baking brownies, the more you practice the basics, the fewer mistakes you will make, and the easier it will get.

Practicing math is as important as practicing sports or musical instruments. You may think that some people have more talent than you and can learn quicker, but practicing anything long enough can make you better. If you dislike math, you probably do what most everyone else does—practice as little as possible. The first thing you must do in preparing for your future goal is to begin practicing math more.

Here are some things you can do to help beat the math monster:

1. Ask your teachers and parents for help.
2. Find a math partner, such as a friend, and have special math meetings to help each other with your math homework.
3. If you have a computer at home, there are special software programs for developing and practicing math skills. Your school or library may have copies of these programs for you to use.
4. Practice with a pocket calculator.
5. Find daily projects that you can do with simple formulas, such as: converting the daytime high temperature from Fahrenheit to Celsius; converting American measurements into metric; converting afternoon and evening times into twenty-four-hour clock times.
6. Math sprints: do the same simple problems every day, racing the clock.
7. Try adding some math problems to your hobbies. If you fly model rockets, you can use math formulas to figure out altitude of rocket flights; if you play baseball, figure out the speed of the ball; or try calculating how much you eat by measuring one spoonful of food.
8. Volunteer to balance your parents' checkbook.
9. Remember that the math monster is only imaginary. If you stop hating it, it won't be a monster anymore.

If you have a computer, try this computer software:

MATH WORD PROBLEMS (Homework Helper), for Apple or IBM computers. For grades seven through twelve.

Spinnaker Software Corporation
One Kendall Square
Cambridge, MA 02139

GEOMETRY, for Apple IIGS or Macintosh computers. For grades nine through twelve.

Broderbund Software
17 Paul Drive
San Rafael, CA 94903

ALGEBRA and ILLUSTRATED GEOMETRY COURSE-MASTER, for Apple II computers. For grades nine through twelve.

Compu-tations, Inc.
P.O. Box 502
Troy, MI 48099

FURTHER READING

Beller, Joel. *So You Want to Do a Science Project!* New York: Arco, 1982.
Burns, Marilyn. *The I Hate Mathematics! Book.* Boston: Little, Brown, 1975.
Gardner, Robert. *Ideas for Science Projects.* New York: Franklin Watts, 1986.
McKay, David W., and Smith, Bruce G. *Space Science Projects for Young Astronauts.* New York: Franklin Watts, 1986.
Moorman, Thomas. *How to Make Your Science Project Scientific.* New York: Atheneum, 1974.
Stoltzfus, John C., and Young, Morris N. *The Complete Guide to Science Fair Competition.* New York: Hawthorne Books, 1972.
Van Deman, Barry A., and McDonald, Ed. *Matter of Fact Guide to Science Fair Projects.* Harwood Heights, Il.: Science Man Press, 1980.

7

Mission 2: Computer Connections

Computers are an important tool for students, engineers, and scientists. They can help make work and learning easier. Every student should have some experience working with a computer by the end of high school.

If you already have a computer, you have a head start. If you don't have a computer, you should be able to use one at your school or public library. Some computer stores will let you use their demonstration models for free. You can also sign up for introductory or advanced computer courses at computer stores or special computer schools.

An excellent way to learn about computers or improve your computer skills is at a computer camp. These summer camps often provide other activities, too, such as swimming or other sports. You won't waste your summer vacation at a computer camp—you'll have fun and get a head start on a future career. For more information about summer camps, see pages 91–98.

Another way to learn about computers is to join a computer group. Almost every city has several of these groups. There is usually at least one group for IBM, Apple, Commodore, Radio Shack, or other computer systems. Computer groups can be very helpful because members usually have answers to problems that you may have in getting your machine to work right or learning how to use software. In addition, members often exchange computer programs and can give you helpful advice on the best programs for your needs.

A computer is more than just a machine. These are some of the different aspects of computers that you can explore:

Hardware. In the early days of personal computers, almost everybody had to be a hardware nut to use one of these machines. Early computer users sometimes used a soldering iron as often as a keyboard. The new generation of hardware, however, does a good job of running itself. You can get by in your computer mission without detailed understanding of computer hardware, but knowing a little about how computers work is always helpful. A book from the library on computers or the instruction manual from a computer company will describe the various parts of the hardware and how they work together.

Word processing. Computer software is a program made of digital instructions that tells the hardware what to do. One type of program is word processing, which is software that lets you use a computer like an intelligent typewriter. You can write reports and essays with word processing and improve your typing, spelling, and organization skills. Most word processing programs are easy to use. Ask for a little help from a teacher or adult, or try a tutorial program and you can be typing away in less than an hour. If you want to make the best use of a word processing program, you can learn to touch-type by taking a course at school. Computer programs that help you teach yourself how to touch-type are also available.

Calculation. Computer programs let you use the power of the microchips to perform simple or complex mathematical functions. Calculation programs make computers work like very powerful pocket calculators. These programs can help you learn more about mathematics or how to solve scientific equations.

Programming. You can learn how to use computers without knowing how to write programs. But if you are interested, this is a valuable skill that will be very useful in almost any career. The most common programming language to begin with is BASIC, but you can also learn LOGO, PASCAL, COBOL, FORTRAN, and many others.

Graphics. Graphics is not the most important computer skill for future astronauts and scientists, but it is fun to learn and to put to use.

The newest graphics programs are also easy to understand and you can begin using them with little practice. Graphics can be used along with word processing and calculation to create illustrations, charts, and graphs.

Games. Computer games are fun, but you can spend so much time playing them that your learning mission will suffer. Games are useful for developing hand-eye coordination and concentration, which can be important for pilots and astronauts. If you do play, don't spend all your time on one game.

Learning programs. These programs are also called tutorials, and they are a practical way to teach yourself. Programs are available in many different subjects, including all of those listed here. If your classroom work is too difficult, try using a special program to catch up. If you already know most of the classwork, try using a special program to move ahead.

Simulators. This may be the best use yet for computer programs. Simulators combine games and learning programs for a fun learning experience. Software simulations are available for atmospheric flight, spaceflight, space station construction, and satellite operations, among others.

Communication. Computers can talk to each other through telephone lines if they are equipped with devices called modems. Modems translate information stored inside the computer into a signal that can be sent from one phone to another. You can use modems to communicate with friends who have computers, call up information sources for answers to questions, and receive messages and useful programs from electronic bulletin board systems (BBS). To find the telephone number of a BBS, ask your local computer store or computer group. Some BBS numbers require long-distance phone calls. If you want to call one of these, remember that calling long distance costs money and you should get permission from your parents or teacher first.

If you are interested in joining an electronic information system, you can write to the following companies for more information.

QUANTUM LINK. This computer "club" was originally created for owners of Commodore computers. It is now available for all major brands of computers. One of the best features about Quantum Link is that it is easy to use. You can use your home or school computer to "talk" to other computer users, especially through special-interest groups that have information about the kind of computer you may be using. You can send messages back and forth, ask for hints about running your computer and software programs, and actually send software programs back and forth. A software library is available through Quantum Link, with thousands of programs that you can copy for your own use (15,000 programs just for Commodore computers!). Quantum Link also offers games with graphics and sound, news services, and an on-line encyclopedia. Registration for Quantum Link costs about ten dollars, and free registration is offered when you buy certain kinds of modems or communication software. The monthly fee is also about ten dollars, and most of the features can be used without paying extra for the time on-line.

For more information:

Quantum Link
8619 Westwood Center Drive
Vienna, VA 22182
1-800-392-8200

PRODIGY. Prodigy is a service sponsored by IBM and Sears. This computerized information source has news, weather, electronic mail, games, daily columns on science, and much more. Of special interest are activity programs that can improve your learning skills. Prodigy costs about ten dollars per month and requires an IBM or Macintosh computer, with at least 512K memory and graphics capability. For more information: 1-800-822-6922.

COMPUSERVE. One of the special features of Compuserve is the "Space Forum," an electronic bulletin board system devoted to aeronautics, aviation, and space travel. Professional scientists and engineers, as well as students and anyone who is interested, can log on to this system to find out what is going on in the space industry. There is a one-time registration fee of about forty dollars to join Compuserve. Charges for connect-time range from six dollars to twelve dollars per hour (ten to twenty-one cents per minute).

For more information:

Compuserve
P.O. Box 20212
Columbus, OH 43220
1-800-848-8199 (outside Ohio)
1-614-457-0802 (in Ohio)

**Computer
Software Choices**

Software companies sometimes upgrade their programs to run on different machines, so if you don't find your machine listed, write for more information. (IBM means IBM-compatible machines. Some programs also require Basic or BASICA to run.) You can write to these companies for catalogs that list all of their software products. If your teacher is interested in other programs or sources of educational software about space science, write for information about the publication *Software for Aerospace Education.*

Educational Technology Office
Educational Affairs Division
Code XET
NASA
Washington, D.C. 20546

For help in writing skills:

ADVENTURES IN SPACE. You can write your own space adventure story using this program. The software lets you choose the action, characters, and details of a NASA spaceship trip. The finished story is six chapters long and can be printed out to make your own book.

Computer systems: Commodore 64, Apple II (64K), or IBM (64K)
Grade levels: 3 to 9
Price: about $40
From: Grolier Electronic Publishing, Inc.
     Sherman Turnpike
     Danbury, CT 06816

For help in designing and flying model rockets:

AERONAUTICS DISK. This software lets you enter specifications for model rockets or hot air balloons. The program will then predict the performance.

Computer systems: Commodore 64/128 (32K), Amiga (512K), or
  IBM PC (640K)
Grade levels: 7 to 12
Price: about $20
From: Science Software
        7370 S. Jay Street
        Littleton, CO 80123

IN SEARCH OF SPACE: INTRODUCTION TO MODEL ROCKETRY. This program is an introduction to the building and launching of model rockets. Text and graphics explain the basics about this subject, including the model rocket safety code. Tests show you how much you have learned.

Computer systems: Apple II (64K)
Grade levels: 4 to 12
Price: about $25
From: Estes Industries
        1295 H Street
        Penrose, CO 81240

For help in learning about astronomy:

ASTRONOMY DISK. You can learn about the principles of astronomy with this program. It is a guide for teaching yourself some of the basic mathematical formulas for orbits, as well as the relationship between different measures of time. You can also use this software to figure the positions of the sun, moon, planets, or stars.

Computer systems: Commodore 64/128 (32K), Amiga (512K), or
  IBM (640K)
Grade levels: 7 to 12
Price: about $35
From: Science Software
        7370 S. Jay Street
        Littleton, CO 80123

COURSE MASTER: BEGIN.ASTRONOMY. This program contains a series of questions and answers about the sun, moon, planets, and space flight. You can test yourself on your understanding of these subjects.

You can also add your own questions and answers to create new tests.

Computer systems: Apple II (48K), Commodore 64/128, or IBM (64K)

Grade levels: 7 to 9

Price: about $30

From: Compu-tations, Inc.
  P.O. Box 502
  Troy, MI 48099

THE EARTH AND MOON SIMULATOR. You can see graphic demonstrations of the orbits of the earth and moon with this program. Simulations re-create the motions of these two objects to show moon phases, tides, and eclipses. A test gives you the opportunity to see how much you have learned.

Computer systems: Apple II (48K)

Grade levels: 5 to 12

Price: about $100

From: Focus Media, Inc.
  P.O. Box 865
  Garden City, NY 11530

INTRODUCTION TO THE HUBBLE SPACE TELESCOPE. The Hubble Space Telescope will be launched by the space shuttle in 1990 or 1991. This program explains how the telescope works and what it will be used for. Both text and graphics are included.

Computer systems: Apple II (48K)

Grade levels: 5 to 8

Price: free

From: NASA Teacher Resource Centers (ask your teacher for help in getting a copy of this software)

PLANETARY CONSTRUCTION SET. You can test your understanding of astronomy, physics, and earth sciences with this program. It lets you create an imaginary planet, including the mass, composition, atmosphere, sun, and satellites. An advanced program challenges you to save an endangered alien life-form by creating a new planet for it.

Computer systems: Apple II (48K)
Grade levels: 8 to adult
Price: about $60
From: Sunburst Communications, Inc.
39 Washington Avenue
Pleasantville, NY 10570

For help in learning more about satellites:

EARTH SATELLITES. If you want to see a satellite in orbit, you can use this program to find out when and where to look. The software calculates this from information you input about the orbiting object, available from amateur astronomy groups, astronomy magazines, and the U.S. Naval Observatory.
Computer systems: Commodore 64/128 (32K), Amiga (512K), or
IBM (640K)
Grade levels: 7 to 12
Price: about $25
From: Science Software
7370 S. Jay Street
Littleton, CO 80123

SAT PLOT. This is another program that tracks satellites in orbit. You can use the program to illustrate satellite paths across the earth's surface.
Computer systems: Atari (32K), IBM (64K, color graphics card)
Grade levels: 9 and up
Price: about $20
From: Tech-Link Incorporated
5075 Bob-O-Link Northwest
North Canton, OH 44720

ORBIT II. This program is a learning game about satellites. To play, you must pick launch speed and launch angle to achieve the right orbit. Graphics show the simulated satellite trajectory and orbit and the effects as you fire thrusters to change course. You can also launch satellites from a space station and simulate the orbit of a real satellite.

Computer systems: Apple II (48K)
Grade levels: 9 to 12
Price: about $25
From: Vernier Software
      2920 S.W. 89th Street
      Portland, OR 97225

For help in learning more about airplanes:

FLIGHT SIMULATOR II. Many home-computer owners already have this popular program, which simulates the control of a single-engine plane. You can take off, maneuver, navigate, and land at many different U.S. airports. The software also lets you change weather conditions to increase the difficulty of a flight.

Computer systems: Commodore 64 (64K), Amiga (512K), Apple
      II (48K), or Atari (64K) (a version for the IBM PC is called Jet)
Grade levels: all
Price: about $50
From: subLOGIC Corporation
      713 Edgebrook Drive
      Champaign, IL 61820

For help in learning more about spacecraft:

ORBITER. Orbiter is a flight simulator for the space shuttle, and lets you control a mission, from takeoff to reentry. Window views, console arrays, instrument readouts, and control panels let you get the feel of a shuttle flight. In orbit, you can also deploy satellites and use the remote manipulator arm. The software also provides unexpected malfunctions to test your responses and awareness of the shuttle systems.

Computer systems: Macintosh (512K) or IBM (256K, 2 360K
      drives, color graphics card)
Grade levels: all
Price: about $50
From: Spectrum Holobyte, Inc.
      2061 Challenger Drive
      Alameda, CA 94501

PROJECT SPACE STATION. You design and build a space station with this software. The process starts with a budget of ten billion dollars, from which you must pay for everything you need. You select a crew from the astronaut biographies that are available in the program. The station parts must be launched into orbit from space shuttles, which you control. The station is put together through extravehicular activity and docking. Some of the problems you may have to face include: if you keep a shuttle in orbit too long, life-support systems may run out; emergencies may change construction schedules; and shuttle landings may cause damage and require repairs.

Computer systems: Apple II (64K), Commodore 64 (64K), or IBM (256K, color graphics card, DOS 3.0)
Grade levels: 7 to adult
Price: about $15
From: *Odyssey,* "The Young People's Magazine of Astronomy and Outer Space"
Order Department
P.O. Box 1612
Waukesha, WI 53187

EARTH ORBIT STATIONS. This program is based on NASA's plans for future space stations. You can choose different levels of play lasting from two to forty hours. In the program, you direct an operation to plan and build a space station. You must work with a budget to create a station from different modules, such as shuttleports, space telescopes, or chemical laboratories. If your plan is successful, you will win profits, which can be used to build more stations. The growth of your space empire will also depend on your understanding of the physical properties and locations of the planets in the solar system.

Computer systems: Commodore 64/128 and Apple II
Grade levels: all
Price: about $40
From: Electronic Arts
1820 Gateway Drive
San Mateo, CA 94404

STARFLIGHT. Starflight is an outer space fantasy game. Your mission is to find colonizable worlds, locate substances or objects of value, and learn the secrets of alien races. Your spacecraft is an interstellar starship with a crew of six, representing five alien races. One of your jobs is to train crew members to use their unique skills and talents and also to work together. On your space mission, you will encounter strange worlds and aliens. Your skill as the commander of this mission will determine whether you successfully colonize new planets or end up in a space war. Starflight has a huge number of star systems and planets stored in its program memory, and you will be able to run thousands of different missions without repeating the same adventure.

Computer systems: IBM and Tandy 1000/2000/3000 (requires 256K, color graphics adapter)
Grade levels: all
Price: about $50
From: Electronic Arts
        1820 Gateway Drive
        San Mateo, CA 94404

For help in learning more about science:

GRAVITY. This is an advanced program that may require a teacher's help. The software simulates the gravitational effects of objects in space. You select the type of object, its mass, speed, and other physical properties. The program demonstrates how the object would be affected by other objects.

Computer systems: IBM (128K)
Grade levels: 9 to adult
Price: about $40
From: Cross Educational Software
        P.O. Box 1536
        Ruston, LA 71270

MICROGRAVITY: AN OPERATION LIFTOFF PROJECT. This software is an introduction to the force of gravity and the mathematical equations that measure it. You can learn about the behavior of objects in orbit and the meaning of escape velocity and orbital velocity. Special tests check your progress.

Computer systems: Apple II (48K)
Grade levels: 5 to 6
Price: about $20
From: NASA Jet Propulsion Laboratory
       Education Outreach Program
       180-205
       4800 Oak Grove Drive
       Pasadena, CA 91103

8

Mission 3: Understanding Space

Astronomy Many astronauts first became interested in space travel because of their curiosity about the stars and planets. Space travel, in fact, has been made possible because of historical interest in these celestial objects, and the development of the science of astronomy. The study of astronomy is very important in space exploration, even though you don't have to be an astronomer to become an astronaut. Learning about the stars and planets gives you an understanding of how celestial objects move, what they are made of, and why it is important to explore them.

The easiest, and most visible, object in the sky that you can learn about is the moon. Even though everybody is used to seeing the moon in the sky, most people do not know why it goes through phases. You can begin your mission by studying the relationship among the earth, moon, and sun. Without a telescope or any special equipment, you can observe the cycles of the moon, lunar eclipses, and the lunar ecliptic (the path the moon takes across the sky). The easiest way to study the moon's cycles is by constructing a scale model using a globe and rubber balls or balloons. If you have a computer, you can also use a software program to simulate the motions of this satellite and other planets in the solar system.

Here are some activities that you can do to learn more about astronomy:

- Build a scale model of the solar system to see how far away from the sun the planets are.
- Read books and magazines on astronomy.
- Join a local amateur astronomy group, or start one of your own.
- If you are a Boy Scout or Girl Scout, study for the astronomy merit badge.
- Learn to find and recognize ten constellations, and make notes about their movement across the sky.
- Read about how scientists use stars to determine time, plot locations on earth, and measure distances on earth.
- If you have a computer, buy or borrow a program that displays sky maps on the screen. Many of these star programs can teach you the movements of stars, how to recognize constellations, locations of planets, times of unusual astronomical events, and the schedules of the rising and setting of stars and planets.

The best astronomy magazine for grades six through twelve is *Odyssey* magazine. It contains articles, illustrations, photos, and explanations about stars, planets, comets, and space exploration. Also, you can keep up-to-date about the space shuttle and participate in writing and art contests. For more information on how to subscribe:

Odyssey magazine
P.O. Box 1612
Waukesha, WI 53187

For interesting posters, educational material, space photographs, books:

Hansen Planetarium Catalog
15 South State Street
Salt Lake City, UT 84111

For educational material, telescopes, science kits, models, science supplies:

Edmund Scientific Catalog
101 East Gloucester Pike
Barrington, NJ 08007

For space shuttle mission patches, photographs, decals, books:

Mail Order Sales Catalog
U.S. Space Education Association
746 Turnpike Road
Elizabethtown, PA 17022-1161

For astronomy books, posters, software, slides, audio tapes, general information on astronomy:

Selectory Catalog
Astronomical Society of the Pacific
1290 24th Avenue
San Francisco, CA 94122

(For an astronomy software catalog, which costs $2, write to the Computer List Department at the address above.)

Planetariums Planetariums are the best place to go to learn how celestial objects move across the sky. There are more than 970 planetariums in the United States. Some planetariums have special programs that use telescopes at night to observe what they have shown through special projections. You can also find other people who are interested in astronomy through local astronomy groups or an astronomy club at your school. Look for amateur astronomy groups and meetings at telescope stores (you will find these listed in the Yellow Pages under Telescopes), planetariums, museums, and colleges.

Model Rockets Building and flying model rockets is a great way to develop your interest in spaceflight. In the last thirty years this hobby has become a major activity for kids around the world, and many adults also participate. Model rockets are made from lightweight cardboard or plastic tubes, with special engines made by several different companies. Kits are sold with everything you need to put together different kinds of rockets, from small single-stage models to scale-model, multi-stage units.

The simplest kits cost less than five dollars and are easy to assemble. Launching equipment is also inexpensive—these kits cost less than ten dollars—or you can design and build your own launch

A model rocket
blasts off. ESTES
INDUSTRIES

platforms. Simple equipment for tracking and measuring rocket flights can be made at home. Computer programs are also available to add to your understanding of the physics of flight. Some programs also let you simulate testing of rocket designs.

The most important part of learning about model rockets is safety.

These miniature rockets are safe when properly used. Understanding and following launch rules is very important. The National Association of Rocketry has devised a list of rules that should be followed by everyone. Some cities have special rocket launching fields that individuals and groups can use, but other cities may not allow rocket launching anywhere. Contact your local rocket group for information about launching, or call your local fire or police department to find out what the regulations are.

If you can't find a local group that sponsors rocket launches, the National Association of Rocketry can help you start your own group. You can also have your Scout troop sponsor a merit badge group, or check with the 4-H Council, Young Astronaut Program, or Civil Air Patrol for other programs.

Here are some activities for learning more about model rockets:

- Get a copy of a book on model rockets from the library or a bookstore. The Boy Scouts also have a merit badge book (*Space Exploration,* published in 1983 by the Boy Scouts of America) that covers model rockets. Read and study it.
- Build a model rocket.
- Learn the safety code for operating model rockets.
- Launch your rocket at an approved launch site. If there is no launching site in your area, contact the National Association of Rocketry, The Young Astronaut Program, or the Civil Air Patrol, and learn what you can do to start your own rocket club and build a launch site.
- Use your rocket launches to learn how to determine rocket altitude, engine thrust, trajectory, flight stability, and other rocket characteristics.

NASA Science Project Programs

NASA sponsors a program for doing advanced science projects in which you may be able to participate. It is called the Shuttle Student Involvement Project for Secondary Schools (SSIP-S). You may have already heard about students who have designed special experiments for this program. The projects that were chosen were sent up on space shuttle flights.

These projects must meet certain requirements for size, power supply, and safety. You can learn more about these requirements, and study the projects that have already been chosen, by writing to NASA. You will probably need some outside help from a teacher or a qualified scientist.

For more information, write to:

SSSIP-S
National Science Teachers Association
1742 Connecticut Avenue NW
Washington, D.C. 20009

NASA Teacher Resource Centers

Many schools and teachers in the United States have already started to learn more about space exploration. NASA and other organizations will provide special materials and programs to teachers to help them teach about space. If you have a teacher who knows a great deal about space exploration, you're in luck. If not, you may be able to help your teacher find out more about space, and learn more yourself at the same time.

NASA Teacher Resource Centers provide NASA publications, lesson plans, teacher guides, classroom activities, laser discs, 35mm slides, audiotapes, and videotapes. Subjects include life science, physical science, space science, computer science, astronomy, chemistry, physics, mathematics, and career guidance.

If you live in these states:	Write to this address:
Alaska, Arizona, California, Hawaii, Idaho, Montana, Nevada, Oregon, Utah, Washington, Wyoming	Teacher Resource Center NASA Ames Research Center Mail Stop 204-7 Moffet Field, CA 94035
Connecticut, Delaware, District of Columbia, Maine, Maryland, Massachusetts, New Hampshire, New Jersey, New York, Pennsylvania, Rhode Island, Vermont	Teacher Resource Center NASA Goddard Space Flight Center New Mail Code 130.0 Greenbelt, MD 20771

Colorado, Kansas, Nebraska, New Mexico, North Dakota, Oklahoma, South Dakota, Texas	Science and Mathematics Teaching Resource Center c/o Education Outreach- SMTRC Mail Stop 520 Pasadena, CA 91109
Florida, Georgia, Puerto Rico, Virgin Islands	Educator Resource Laboratory NASA John F. Kennedy Space Center Mail Code ERL Kennedy Space Center, FL 32899
Kentucky, North Carolina, South Carolina, Virginia, West Virginia	Teacher Resource Center NASA Langley Research Center Mail Stop 146 Hampton, VA 23665
Illinois, Indiana, Michigan, Minnesota, Ohio, Wisconsin	Teacher Resource Center NASA Lewis Research Center Mail Stop 8-1 Cleveland, OH 44135
Alabama, Arkansas, Iowa, Louisiana, Mississippi, Missouri, Tennessee	Teacher Resource Center NASA Marshall Space Flight Center Huntsville, AL 35807

NASA also offers Telelecture Programs for schools. Modern technology is used in this program to present "live" but remote programs by NASA experts. A telephone conference call connects the speaker with a class, and while the talk is being given, the teacher shows slides that illustrate the subject. Because there is a two-way phone hookup, you can also ask questions of the experts. This service is free but requires advance registration. Telelecture programs offered are "Air Transportation of the Future," "Wind Tunnels: The Basic Tools of Aeronautical Research," "Careers in Aerospace," "Overview of NASA Langley Research Center," "Exploration of the Solar System," "Voyage to the Outer Planets," "Planetary Exploration through the Year 2000," "Manned Spaceflight," "The Space Shuttle," "Science in Space," "The Space Station," "Satellites at Work," and "Spaceflight: The Next Probable Steps."

For more information, write to:

Telelecture Programs
NASA Visitor Center
Langley Research Center
Mail Stop 480
Hampton, VA 23665-5225

Civil Air Patrol

Congress established the Civil Air Patrol (CAP) as the official auxiliary organization for the United States Air Force. The CAP provides emergency services, trains cadets, and is a great source of information about aerospace subjects. The CAP has many different publications and educational materials for elementary through high school students. These include biographies of famous aviators, explanations of the space shuttle, principles of flight, posters, and activity guides. Local CAP officers also give lectures and demonstrations on topics related to flight and space exploration. Your teacher can find out more about these services from:

Civil Air Patrol
Aerospace Education
HQ CAP/EDF
Maxwell AFB, AL 36112-5572

Space Museums

You can visit many places in the United States to see exhibits and displays about the exploration of space. The history of flight, rockets, and spacecraft is an important part of understanding how the space program works, and what future spacecraft will look like. You will also better understand astronomy and space science when you can see displays, demonstrations, and hands-on exhibits.

You may be able to visit nearby museums and aerospace facilities with school groups or as part of other organized groups such as the Young Astronauts or Boy Scouts. Most facilities that are open to the public will also arrange guided tours and demonstrations.

If you are on vacation with your family, you might be able to visit some of these places. Your parents might even be willing to plan vacations to include important facilities—after all, such visits are educational.

When visiting museums, remember to ask about special programs, summer camps, and student projects. Many science museums offer very interesting activities that you may be able to participate in if you live in the area. Also, museums often have volunteer programs. As a volunteer, you may get to work on special exhibits or demonstrations or get training to be an "explainer" for visitors. Following are a few of the interesting aerospace museums and centers. You can write to the addresses listed to get information on visiting hours, admission price, and a description of their facilities.

Aerospace Historical Center. The Aerospace Museum includes special displays of eighty-eight heroes of the history of flight in the International Aerospace Hall of Fame.

Aerospace Historical Center
Balboa Park
San Diego, CA 92101
619-234-8291

Alabama Space and Rocket Center. This is the world's largest space museum. Artifacts on display include full-size rockets such as the Redstone, Titan 2, German V-2, Jupiter, Juno 1, Saturn 5, and Saturn 1B. A guided bus tour includes the NASA Marshall Center, outdoor simulators, and Omnimax theater. Other displays include an external fuel tank from the space shuttle, mock-ups of Spacelab and Skylab, a replica of the Apollo Lunar Landing Module, Lunar Rover, satellites, Apollo 16, Mercury 7, and a model of the Hubble Space Telescope.

Alabama Space and Rocket Center
Tranquility Base
Huntsville, AL 35807
205-837-3400

Air Force Space Museum. This museum is located at the birthplace of the U.S. manned space program, Launch Complex 26 at Cape Canaveral. Rockets on display include a German V-1, Mercury Redstone, Atlas, and Titan ICBM. A driving tour of the museum includes views of launch areas that are still in use.

Air Force Space Museum
Eastern Space and Missile Center
Patrick AFB, FL 32925

California Museum of Science and Industry. This museum has a large collection of aircraft, from a model of Leonardo Da Vinci's ornithopter to a Saturn V rocket. Other displays include satellites, the Apollo-Soyuz mission, the space shuttle, and the Apollo lunar expedition.

California Museum of Science and Industry
700 State Drive
Los Angeles, CA 90037
213-744-7400

Center of Science and Industry. This science museum has many exhibits and demonstrations that illustrate how the various branches of science work. Visitors can also view a NASA space trainer, satellites, a Gemini capsule, and an Apollo capsule.

Center of Science and Industry
280 E. Broad Street
Columbus, OH 43215
614-228-6361

Franklin Institute. Many different vehicles are on display in the Hall of Aviation. Included are one of the Wright Brothers' early airplanes, a T-33 trainer, Link trainer, and hundreds of scale models showing the history of flight.

Franklin Institute Science Museum and Planetarium
Philadelphia, PA 19103
215-448-1200

Kansas Cosmosphere and Discovery Center. Along with an Omnimax theater, which shows spectacular 70mm films, the center has a Hall of Space that includes command modules from the Mercury,

Gemini, and Apollo flights; the first rocket flown by rocket pioneer Robert Goddard; a German V-2 rocket engine; replicas of the Soviet Sputnik satellite and the U.S. Explorer I satellite; moon rocks; tools used by the Apollo crew on the lunar surface; and many other space devices. This space center also has hands-on exhibits, including a lunar module cockpit that takes you through a simulated lunar landing.

The Kansas Cosmosphere and Discovery Center
1100 N. Plum
Hutchinson, KS 67501

Museum of Science and Space Transit Planetarium. The planetarium at this museum is the largest of its type. Special shows include simulations of spacecraft operation in space, including docking maneuvers that visitors are allowed to control.

Museum of Science and Space Transit Planetarium
3280 S. Miami Avenue
Miami, FL 33129
305-854-4247 (museum)   305-854-2222 (planetarium)

Museum of Science and Industry. On display at this museum is the Apollo 8 spacecraft, the first vehicle to carry people to the moon. Other space exhibits include computer simulations of lunar landings and planetary exploration.

Museum of Science and Industry
Chicago, IL 60637
312-684-1414

National Air and Space Museum. This is the most popular museum in the world. It includes everything from the first airplane ever flown to full-size rockets from the early days of U.S. spaceflight. One exhibit demonstrates the importance of computer-aided design in the development of aircraft.

National Air and Space Museum
Sixth Street and Independence Avenue
Washington, D.C. 20560
202-357-2700

Neil Armstrong Air and Space Museum. The Gemini 8 capsule, which Armstrong—the first man to walk on the moon—and David Scott rode in 1966, is on display, along with other space artifacts. Films and videotapes illustrate the history of the U.S. space program.

Neil Armstrong Air and Space Museum
Interstate Highway 75
Wapakoneta, OH 45895
419-738-8811

The U.S. Air Force Museum. This museum has one of the largest displays of military aircraft in the world. The collection of vintage planes is varied, and ranges from one of the Wright Brothers' early models to the latest jet fighters. Spacecraft at the museum include a Titan 1 ICBM, a Mercury capsule, a Gemini capsule, an Apollo 15 capsule, and the X-15, X-24A, and X-24B experimental aircraft.

U.S. Air Force Museum
Wright-Patterson Air Force Base
Dayton, OH 45433
513-255-3284

The U.S. Naval Aviation Museum. The aircraft on display here range from the earliest Navy planes to the latest. A display shows the history of aircraft engines, from early internal combustion models to jet engines. Visitors can also see spacecraft, including the Skylab 1 command module.

U.S. Naval Aviation Museum
U.S. Naval Air Station
Pensacola, FL 32508
904-452-3606

NASA Visitor Centers

Many of the NASA centers have visitor exhibits, tours, and special programs that can be very educational for future astronauts. Visits to NASA centers may be possible through such groups as the Boy or Girl Scouts, Young Astronauts, or school organizations. You may even be able to talk your parents into planning a vacation trip to one or more of these places, because the centers are just as interesting for adults.

Langley Research Center. This center has forty exhibits, including the evolution of air travel, the Apollo 12 command module, a model of the space shuttle Columbia, and films on aeronautical and space themes.

Langley Research Center
NASA Visitor Center
Mail Stop 580
Hampton, VA 23665
804-864-6000

Dryden Flight Research Facility. The Dryden visitor center has a thirty-minute film that introduces you to the work of the facility. Also at this location is a museum of flight with aircraft on display, including an F-18, a C-140, an F-15, and the experimental Hymat. A tour takes you through some of the projects that are under way.

Dryden Flight Research Facility
Edwards Air Force Base, CA 93523
805-258-3346

Goddard Space Flight Center. More than six thousand scientists, engineers, and staff members work at this large NASA center. Goddard is responsible for monitoring rocket launches around the world and calculating orbits for piloted missions. Communications from satellites and astronauts in orbit are first received at Goddard before being translated from their digitized computer form and sent to other NASA centers. Visitors to Goddard can tour the museum, which has twenty-five satellites and spacecraft on display.

NASA/Goddard Visitor Information Center and Museum
Greenbelt, MD 20771
301-286-8981

Johnson Space Center. Johnson Space Center is the main headquarters for NASA space programs. Currently on display are the Faith 7 Mercury capsule, Gemini capsule, Apollo 7 capsule, Moon Buggy, lunar module, Saturn 5 rocket, Mercury Redstone rocket, and the mobile quarantine trailer used when the Apollo astronauts first returned from the moon.

In preparation for a flight aboard the Space Shuttle Columbia, astronaut Thomas K. Mattingly takes part in a simulation of activity in the Johnson Space Center's motion base simulator.
NASA

Johnson Space Center
Houston, TX 77058
713-483-4321

Kennedy Space Center. This is where you go if you want to see a space shuttle launch. You can walk right in—reservations are not necessary. Visitor tours include the Operations and Checkout Building, Flight Crew Training Building, and Vehicle Assembly Building (one of the largest buildings in the world). Display vehicles include a Saturn Apollo rocket, a mobile launcher, space shuttle transport, and an operational lunar module.

Kennedy Space Center Visitor Center
Kennedy Space Center, FL 32899
407-452-2121

Lewis Research Center. Visitors see a film, planetary exploration displays, satellites, a model of the space station, and an Apollo capsule. A guided tour includes visits to two facilities where work is being done on zero-gravity and propulsion systems.

Girl Scouts take a guided tour of an aerospace plant.
GIRL SCOUTS OF THE U.S.A.

NASA Lewis Research Center Visitor Information Center
Cleveland, OH 44135
216-433-2000

National Space Technology Laboratories. This NASA center includes educational displays on space, oceans, and earth. The tour takes visitors to the laboratories where shuttle engines are test fired.

National Space Technology Laboratories
Bay Saint Louis, MS 39529
601-688-2370

Jet Propulsion Laboratory. Visitors are only allowed on special tour days. A two-hour tour includes a visit to the museum, with its displays of spacecraft models, and a multimedia show about the work done at JPL. A tour takes visitors to the spacecraft assembly building, where payloads are put together, and the viewing gallery of Mission Control, where spacecraft in orbit are monitored.

Jet Propulsion Laboratory
Pasadena, CA 91109
818-354-2337

Chartrand, Mark. *Skyguide:* (A Golden Field Guide Set). New York: Golden Press, 1982.

Menzel, Donald H. *A Field Guide to the Stars and Planets* (Peterson Field Guide Series). Boston: Houghton Mifflin, 1975.

Schwartz, Julius. *Earthwatch: Space-Time Investigations with a Globe.* New York: McGraw-Hill, 1977.

Simon, Seymour. *Look to the Night Sky: An Introduction to Star Watching.* New York: Penguin, 1979.

Stine, G. Harry. *Handbook of Model Rocketry* (5th edition). New York: Arco, 1983.

9

Mission 4: Joining Groups

You will find support for your ambitions to be an astronaut by joining groups that promote space travel, science, or aerospace education. You may already be a member of a group such as the Boy Scouts or Girl Scouts, which have special programs about space. Other groups are more specialized, such as the Young Astronauts. Some groups are part of professional organizations of scientists and teachers, and provide up-to-date information on research and technology.

Joining one or more of these groups is a good way to further your science education. If a group that interests you does not have a local chapter, you can start one by yourself, with the help of friends or teachers. Also, by volunteering your time to some groups, you will get valuable experience in working with other people who have similar ambitions, and develop important adult connections for future college plans. Following are some groups that you can join to pursue your interest in space exploration.

Young Astronaut Program. The Young Astronaut Program has been in existence for only a few years, but there are already hundreds of thousands of members. Chapters are usually formed through elementary and junior high schools, but anyone is eligible to join this exciting program. Young Astronauts was organized to increase interest in math and science, because these subjects are very important for space exploration.

Being a Young Astronaut gives you the opportunity to meet astronauts, scientists, and experts in space development; learn about scientific principles important to space flight; and join in activities such as building and launching model rockets. The Young Astronaut Program has special buttons and badges for members and sponsors contests in which the winners get free trips to NASA launches and U.S. Space Camp. Membership levels are:

	Grades	Rank 1	Rank 2	Rank 3
Trainee	1–3	Pledge	Cadet	Cadet Leader
Pilot	4–6	Co-Pilot	Pilot	Captain
Commander	7–9	Ship Commander	Squadron Commander	Star Commander

As a Young Astronaut, you can be promoted from one rank to the next by performing certain activities and meeting the requirements set by your chapter leader. Special contests and competitions will allow you to develop skills and knowledge that can be useful to you in school and in your future career. The prizes for winning these contests are scholarships, merchandise, and free trips to meet astronauts and scientists and see rocket launches.

What do you do at Young Astronaut chapter meetings?

- Meet scientists, engineers, and teachers who share information with you.
- Take trips to planetariums and museums.
- Take trips to places where high-tech research and space-development projects are under way.
- Participate in a space watch for astronomical events.
- Learn about the latest developments in space exploration.
- Perform experiments that demonstrate scientific principles that are important in understanding gravity, momentum, propulsion, and other properties.
- Build and launch model rockets.

The Young Astronaut Program also has a special computer communication service called "Astronet." You can connect any computer to Astronet with a modem and telephone. If you don't have a computer, ask for permission to use your school computer. Astronet has a menu that offers different levels of access, based on your Young Astronaut membership level. Information available includes updates on the space program, news about Young Astronaut activities and contests, a continuing story about Young Astronaut adventures called "Space Camp Alpha," and games for you to play.

Young Astronauts also receive *Young Astronaut,* the official newsletter of the Young Astronaut Council. This monthly publication has news about Young Astronaut activities, contests, interviews with astronauts, articles about space and astronaut training, puzzles, NASA news, and computers.

If there is no Young Astronaut chapter in your area, you can start one of your own. The Young Astronaut Council will send information that will help you find other interested kids, get assistance from teachers and parents, and join the national organization. For more information, write to:

The Young Astronaut Council
1015 15th Street NW, Suite 905
Washington, DC 20005

The Space Camp Club. One of the most popular programs among future astronauts is the U.S. Space Camp at NASA's Marshall Space Flight Center in Huntsville, Alabama. The camp offers more than just the training program, however. You can participate in the Space Camp Club, a home-study course for students from ages nine to sixteen. Space Camp Club will keep you informed about developments in space exploration and help you understand what future career opportunities in space exist.

Special mailings feature activities that explain the history of space flight, how people can survive in space, and how you can prepare yourself for space travel. Step-by-step instructions teach you how to prepare for space missions and perform experiments. Space Camp Club also has a newsletter that links members across the country. There are two types of membership: Level I is for ages nine to thirteen, Level II is for ages fourteen to sixteen. Membership costs fifteen dollars. For more information, write to:

Space Camp Club
P.O. Box 1287
Huntsville, AL 35807

Boy Scouts of America. The Boy Scouts is an organization that teaches good citizenship, practical skills, and leadership. Many astronauts have been Boy Scouts.

Boy Scouts can study aerospace by earning the Space Exploration Merit Badge and the Astronomy Merit Badge. Explorer Scouts can also participate in Project POSTAR, a program sponsored by the Boy Scouts and NASA. Scouts in the program can create experiments that may be selected as part of future space shuttle payloads.

To find the Boy Scout troop or Explorer post closest to your neighborhood, call your local Boy Scout Council. The telephone number will be in the phone book, listed under "Boy Scouts of America."

Girl Scouts of the U.S.A. The Girl Scouts is the largest volunteer organization for girls in the world. There are more than three hundred local councils in cities across the country. Girl Scouts can assist you in learning more about future careers and developing useful skills— and you'll have fun at the same time. The Girl Scout handbooks and *Girl Scout Badges and Signs* offer activities and guides for many subjects that relate to science and space careers.

To find the closest Girl Scout troop, call your local Girl Scout Council. The telephone number will be in the phone book, listed under "Girl Scouts."

United States Space Foundation. The purpose of the United States Space Foundation is to "help shape America's future in space for the benefit of all." This group aims to help establish a space program, help teachers improve the quality of math and science education, and increase awareness of the beneficial uses of space.

Members of the United States Space Foundation include astronauts, scientists, politicians, teachers, and students from elementary school to college. You can join this organization for only five dollars if you are in elementary school and ten dollars if you are in junior or senior high school. Members receive a monthly newsletter called *Spacewatch,* which gives information about space developments, politics, and activities related to space education. For more information, write to:

United States Space Foundation
P.O. Box 1838
Colorado Springs, CO 80901

Spaceweek. First held in 1980, Spaceweek is celebrated every year on the anniversary of the Apollo 11 lunar landing, July 16–24, 1969. In many cities in the United States, Spaceweek activities include displays, lectures, and demonstrations by scientists, engineers, and astronauts. The event is planned by volunteers who meet throughout the year to organize activities, working together with Spaceweek headquarters in Houston, which provides posters, suggestions, and information about getting started. You can help by volunteering with your local Spaceweek group, or starting your own Spaceweek group if there isn't one in your area. For more information, write to:

Spaceweek National Headquarters
P.O. Box 58172
Houston, TX 77258

The American Radio Relay League. A great way to get involved with electronics and communications technology is to become an amateur radio operator. You can start at any age to learn about this hobby, also known as "ham radio." With a short-wave radio and an operator's license, you can talk to other amateur radio operators around the world. Unlike CB radio operators (citizen's band), who are restricted to short-range transmissions, "hams" are able to send and receive messages from anywhere, and often help out during disasters by relaying important information.

Amateur radio teaches you about science. For instance, you can learn to bounce radio signals off the moon or meteors to gain extra distance. OSCAR-1, the first satellite for amateur radio operators, was launched in 1961, allowing operators to reach more distant locations. This satellite was built by ham operators in a garage. Nine other satellites for hams have been launched since then. Computers are also important to amateur radio operation, sending digital messages from one radio to another.

In 1983, astronaut Owen Garriott became the first ham operator to send and receive messages from space. Other hams include King Hussein of Jordan and Senator Barry Goldwater of Arizona. Hams can be any age, but you must take a test before you can get your amateur radio license. You can also join a special group for free, the Archie Radio Club. With membership, you get a copy of *Archie's Ham Radio Adventure,* a subscription to *Archie Radio Club News,* and an information chart that will help locate radio bands to listen to. For membership information, write to:

Archie Radio Club
c/o American Radio Relay League
225 Main Street
Newington, CT 06111

National Association of Rocketry (NAR). You can build and fly model rockets just by purchasing model kits from your local hobby store. Such groups as the Young Astronauts also use model rockets as part of their programs. If you want to learn more, or participate in advanced rocketry experiments, you should join the National Association of Rocketry.

This group is the largest model rocketry and spacemodeling organization in the world. It sponsors national and international contests, publishes a monthly magazine called *American Spacemodeling,* and sets up the safety regulations for launching model rockets. *American Spacemodeling* has rocket plans, articles about building and launching model rockets, and information about improving the performance of rockets. Members of the NAR also get discounts on decals, jacket patches, books, model plans, posters, and other model rocket products.

About sixty model rocket clubs in the United States are members of the NAR. If there is no club in your area, you can start one with information and help from the national office of the NAR. One of the important benefits that the NAR provides for its clubs is low-cost insurance for model rocket launchings. Most cities and towns in this country will not let you launch model rockets without this insurance because of the possibility of personal or property damage. Joining the NAR will help you learn safe procedures for launchings and satisfy local government requirements for insurance. For more information, write to:

National Association of Rocketry
2140 Colburn Drive
Shakopee, MN 55379

National Space Society. This group promotes interest in space through publications, lobbying, meetings, and activities. Members receive a monthly magazine, *Space World*. For more information, write to:

National Space Society
600 Maryland Avenue SW, Suite 203 West
Washington, DC 20024

Students for the Exploration and Development of Space (SEDS). SEDS is an organization for high school and college students. Most of its work is done through chapters, which are usually located at colleges and universities. SEDS is a great resource for meeting other serious and advanced students. The organization also provides useful information about space research and aerospace resources. Write to SEDS for information about chapters in your area:

SEDS
77 Massachusetts Avenue W20-445
Cambridge, MA 02139

10

Mission 5: Hands-on Vacations

One of the most exciting summer vacation adventures is a trip to one of the space camps around the country. They have become popular through word-of-mouth, with participants passing the excitement to their friends and classmates. Also, thousands of kids have learned about space camps from the 1986 movie, *Spacecamp,* and through the Young Astronaut Program.

Space camps offer hands-on learning about space shuttle operations by using simulators, computers, and mock-ups. Space campers study shuttle operations, plan launches, and carry out realistic space missions, with designated pilots, crew members, and mission controllers.

Going to a space camp will not guarantee you a job as an astronaut, but it can help increase your understanding about how the shuttle works. You can also learn about the other jobs needed to launch and fly these spacecraft and the teamwork necessary for successful missions.

Future Astronaut Training Program

What: Level I is a five-day session that trains astronaut candidates to carry out a simulated shuttle mission. Level II is a three-day session that trains for an advanced shuttle mission, followed by a two-day visit to NASA's Johnson Space Center in Houston. Level II astronaut candidates must be graduates of the Level I program.

Sessions are open to boys and girls entering the seventh, eighth, or ninth grades.

Where: Kansas Cosmosphere and Space Center, Hutchinson, Kansas

When: sessions held from late May through late July

Details: Housing and meals are provided, with adult supervision. Instructors are from the science education staff of the Kansas Cosmosphere and Space Center. All astronaut candidates receive a flight jacket, data manual, official camp T-shirt, and astronaut wings. Level II participants also receive a book about the NASA Mars mission.

LEVEL I

Day One. Astronaut candidates learn about the space environment, life-support equipment, spacecraft design, space foods, and the problems of zero-gravity bathrooms. Activities include physical exercises that help condition the body for the effects of zero-gravity, handling space suits, and testing programs like those used for NASA astronauts.

Day Two. Campers study space flight and rocket propulsion, measure the power of rocket engines, and build and launch model rockets. The model rocket program is used to learn and practice methods for measuring the altitude, speed, and trajectory of the rockets.

Day Three. Astronaut candidates study the space shuttle and practice for shuttle missions—including eating a meal of space food. A special aircraft flight simulator is used to experience the sensations of flying an airplane. Another simulator provides the feel of the Manned Maneuvering Unit (MMU), which NASA astronauts use as a life-support system and propulsion unit when performing extravehicular activities in space. Also, a live teleconference is held with a NASA astronaut.

Day Four. Campers practice for the final mission. The flight crew practices in the Falcon space shuttle simulator to rehearse the launch and piloting controls, and the mission control crew practices on a ground-control simulator for their role during the mission. A planetarium show explores the night sky, and telescopes are used to view celestial objects and actual satellites.

Day Five. Each astronaut team carries out a shuttle mission, including launch, deployment of satellites, scientific experiments, reentry, landing, debriefing, and mission analysis. Following completion of the mission, the crew is awarded astronaut wings and certificates at graduation ceremonies.

LEVEL II

Day One through Day Three. Graduates of the Level I program receive advanced briefings on the future of the U.S. space program. Future projects such as the space station and a Mars mission are discussed, and students learn about different careers in space. Students train on the simulators for an advanced shuttle mission, which takes place on the third day.

Days Four and Five. After debriefing from their shuttle mission, students travel as a group to Houston for a special visit to the Johnson

Space campers watch a rocket launch. SPACE CEN- TER, ALAMOGORDO, NEW MEXICO

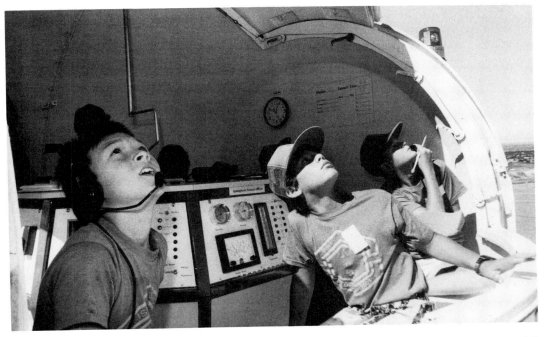

A space camp cadet tries on a space suit.
SPACE CENTER, ALAMOGORDO, NEW MEXICO

Space Center. At JSC, the group receives briefings by NASA astronauts and officials. A guided tour of the JSC facility allows close inspection of the mock-ups built for the Skylab and space station missions. The trip ends with a banquet featuring former astronauts, who speak about their space careers. After returning to the Cosmosphere in Hutchinson, students attend a graduation ceremony, and each graduate is awarded an advanced level certificate and gold astronaut wings. For more information, write to:

Kansas Cosmosphere and Space Center
c/o Future Astronaut Training Program
1100 N. Plum
Hutchinson, KS 67501

United States Space Camp

What: Space Camp is a five-day program for fourth through seventh graders. Space Academy Level I is a program for eighth, ninth, and tenth graders. Space Academy Level II is a longer program, ten days, for eleventh and twelfth graders plus college freshmen. A special Space Academy program is also available for teachers and adults.

Where: near NASA's Marshall Space Flight Center in Huntsville, Alabama

When: March through summer months.

Details: Housing and meals are provided, with adult supervision. Counselors are university students with majors in engineering or education. Campers receive an official Space Camp T-shirt and training manual.

LEVEL I

Day One. Campers learn about rocketry and propulsion, and build their own model rockets. A tour of the nearby rocket park illustrates the history of the U.S. rocket program.

Day Two. Activities introduce campers to life-support systems used in space, including food and waste management. Spacesuits, helmets, and backpack systems for EVA (extravehicular activity) are demonstrated. There is a tour of the NASA training center for Skylab astronauts.

Day Three. Demonstrations and experiments show the effects of zero-gravity and low gravity on the lunar surface. Equipment used includes a "moon walk trainer" and the Multi-Axis Trainer, which is like a jungle gym and a merry-go-round combined. Campers experience simulated weightlessness in a swimming pool and take a tour of NASA's neutral buoyancy tank.

Day Four. Campers launch model rockets, study computer programs, and learn about future careers in space and space technology.

Day Five. Campers are chosen for space shuttle and mission control crews for simulated missions. Each mission includes countdown, launch, orbit, and reentry. Graduation ceremonies are held following the mission, with Space Camp wings awarded to campers.

LEVEL II

Day One. Campers learn about shuttle design and operation by using cockpit and ground-control simulators. A Spacelab mock-up enables them to conduct scientific experiments.

Day Two. Campers are divided into teams with special assignments to prepare for a simulated shuttle mission. Activities are designed to familiarize campers with shuttle crew and ground-support requirements. Demonstrations include trying on space suits and EVA equipment.

Day Three. This day is devoted to learning about shuttle payloads and deployment. Training covers satellite technology, use of the remote arm, conducting scientific experiments in space, and construction of a space structure in simulated weightless conditions.

Day Four. A simulated shuttle mission begins, with countdown and launch, followed by maneuvering to achieve orbit objectives. Ground support includes tracking and monitoring shuttle activity. Shuttle and ground-support teams conduct experiments to compare the effects of space on biological systems. A docking simulation is carried out with a space station, and ground-support crews exchange places with the shuttle crew.

Day Five. Team members switch positions and analyze the mission during a debriefing session. They learn about the ground-based preparations of the shuttle between missions. The final activity is a graduation ceremony, which awards certificates and Space Camp wings to campers. For more information, write to:

United States Space Camp
The Space and Rocket Center
Tranquility Base
Huntsville, AL 35807

Shuttle Camp 2001

What: A week-long program for third through ninth graders. Sessions are offered days only for third and fourth graders (no housing) and full-time for fifth through ninth graders.

Where: International Space Hall of Fame, Alamagordo, New Mexico

When: June and July

Details: Housing and meals are provided for full-time sessions, with adult supervision.

Campers study space careers, the history of spaceflight, problems of living in space, computers, computer communications, science experiments, robotics, astronomy, and astronaut survival training. Experiments with model rockets involve launching payloads and using instrumentation to track rocket flights. Simulators are available for use, and hands-on training includes weightless simulation under water. Campers build weather stations, see planetarium shows, and

Young space campers undergo weightless training in this pool.
SPACE CENTER, ALAMOGORDO, NEW MEXICO

make observations with telescopes. A special feature of Shuttle Camp 2001 is its location. Field trips take campers to real astronaut training sites and the rocket testing site at White Sands Missile Range (some campers have even been allowed to push the button to launch live rocket engine tests). Lectures and seminars by space experts are also offered.

For more information:

Shuttle Camp 2001
P.O. Box 533
Alamagordo, NM 88311-0533
1-800-545-4021 (outside New Mexico)
1-800-634-6438 (in New Mexico)

Would-be astronauts study model rockets and shuttles at Shuttle Camp 2001, Alamogordo, New Mexico. SPACE CENTER, ALAMOGORDO, NEW MEXICO

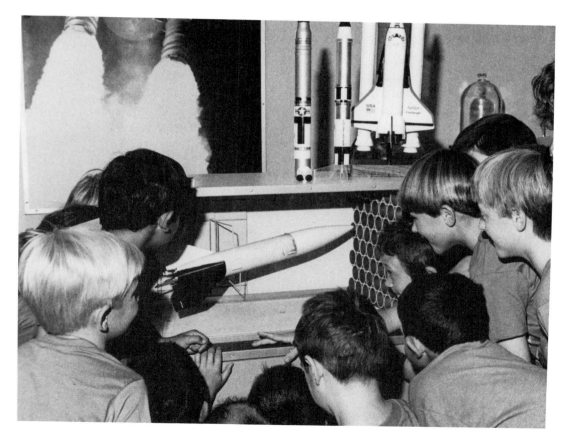

11

Mission 6: Physical Fitness

Exercise and fitness are important to your astronaut training program. You must pass certain fitness tests before you can be accepted for astronaut training, either as an astronaut pilot, mission specialist, or payload specialist. Why? People who are fit and healthy can work more efficiently and longer without problems. Being fit also keeps people healthy, no matter what their career is.

You should start now to develop good exercise habits. You can play on sports teams or work out by yourself. It is not necessary to become a "jock" or super athlete, just to become fit.

The following are goals with which you can compare yourself to others your age. These standards are set by the Presidential Physical Fitness Award Program. If your scores are equal to or higher than the scores listed, you qualify for a Presidential Physical Fitness Award certificate, signed by the President of the United States. Students who qualify for this award also receive a special emblem, which can be worn on sweaters, jackets, or sweatsuits.

If your school doesn't yet participate in this program, ask your teacher or principal to write for more information:

President's Council on Physical Fitness and Sports
450 5th Street NW
Washington, DC 20001

Curl-Ups   **Objective:** Number of curl-ups performed in one minute

Equipment: Stopwatch and a mat or other clean surface

Starting position: Lie on your back with your knees flexed at ninety degrees. Have a partner hold your feet. Your heels should not be more than twelve inches from your buttocks, and your back should be flat on the floor. Cross your arms with hands placed on opposite shoulders, arms close to your chest. Keep your arms in contact with your chest at all times.

Action: Raise your trunk, curling up to touch your elbows to your thighs. Then lower your back to the floor until your upper back touches the floor.

The test: The timer calls out the signal "Go" and begins timing for one minute. At the end of sixty seconds, the timer calls out "Stop." Your score is the number of correct curl-ups finished in sixty seconds.

Rules: 1. "Bouncing" off the floor or mat is not allowed. 2. A curl-up is only correct if you: a) keep your fingers touching your shoulders; b) touch your elbows to your thighs; c) touch your upper back to the floor before beginning the next curl-up.

Pull-Ups   **Objective:** Maximum number of pull-ups completed (no time limit)

Equipment: A horizontal bar at a height that you can hang from with your arms fully extended and your feet not touching the floor

Starting position: Hang from the bar with an overhand grasp (palms facing away from your body). A partner can help lift you up to grasp the bar before you start.

Action: Raise your body until your chin is over the bar without touching it and then lower your body to the full-hang starting position.

The test: Complete as many pull-ups as possible.

Rules: 1. Your body must not swing. If your body starts to swing, your partner can stop the swinging by holding an arm across the front of your thighs. 2. The pull-up must be smooth and not a snapping or jerky movement. Kicking the legs or bending the knees is not permitted.

V-Sit Reach   **Objective:** Farthest distance reached past the baseline

Equipment: A clean floor, a yardstick, and adhesive tape

Set-up: Mark a straight line two feet long on the floor with tape for the baseline. Draw a line perpendicular (ninety degrees) to the center of the baseline and two feet long on each side. This is the measuring line. Draw one-inch and half-inch marks on the measuring line from the point where the measuring line intersects the baseline.

Starting position: Remove your shoes and sit on the floor with the measuring line between your legs. The soles of your feet should be just behind the baseline. Your heels should be eight to twelve inches apart.

Action: Clasp your thumbs together with your palms down and place them on the floor between your legs. Have a partner hold your legs flat on the floor and flex your feet so that they are perpendicular to the floor. Slowly reach forward as far as possible along the measuring line with your fingers touching the floor. You can take three practice tries. On the fourth try, hold your farthest reach for a count of three seconds. Your score is the distance from the baseline to your fingertips.

Rules: 1. Your legs must remain straight and the soles of your feet must be perpendicular to the floor. 2. Don't bounce. 3. Your score is marked at the point where your fingertips touch the floor. 4. Scores are recorded as "plus" scores if you reach past the baseline and "minus" scores if you can't reach the baseline. All scores are recorded to the nearest half inch.

One Mile Run/Walk

Objective: Fastest time to cover a distance of one mile

Equipment: Stopwatch and a track or safe running area marked for a distance of one mile

Starting position: Take a "ready" position at the start of the course.

Action: At the signal "Ready, Go," begin running. Walking is permitted if you cannot run the whole distance.

Rules: Walking is permitted, but you should try to cover the distance in as short a time as possible.

Shuttle Run

Objective: Fastest time

Equipment: Stopwatch, adhesive tape or chalk, two blocks of wood about two inches by two inches by four inches (or two erasers)

Set-up: Mark or tape two lines on the floor, thirty feet apart. The

Age	Curl-Ups	Shuttle Run (seconds)	V-Sit Reach (inches)	One Mile Run (min:sec)	Pull-Ups
		Boys			
6	33	12.1	+3.5	10:15	2
7	36	11.5	+3.5	9:22	4
8	40	11.1	+3.0	8:48	5
9	41	10.9	+3.0	8:31	5
10	45	10.3	+4.0	7:57	6
11	47	10.0	+4.0	7:32	6
12	50	9.8	+4.0	7:11	7
13	53	9.5	+3.5	6:50	7
14	56	9.1	+4.5	6:26	10
15	57	9.0	+5.0	6:20	11
16	56	8.7	+6.0	6:08	11
17	55	8.7	+7.0	6:06	13

Age	Curl-Ups	Shuttle Run (seconds)	V-Sit Reach (inches)	One Mile Run (min:sec)	Pull-Ups
		Girls			
6	32	12.4	+5.5	11:20	2
7	34	12.1	+5.0	10:36	2
8	38	11.8	+4.5	10:02	2
9	39	11.1	+5.5	9:30	2
10	40	10.8	+6.0	9:19	3
11	42	10.5	+6.5	9:02	3
12	45	10.4	+7.0	8:23	2
13	46	10.2	+7.0	8:13	2
14	47	10.1	+8.0	7:59	2
15	48	10.0	+8.0	8:08	2
16	45	10.1	+9.0	8:23	1
17	44	10.0	+8.0	8:15	1

lines should be parallel. Place the blocks behind one line and use the other line as the starting line.

Action: On the signal "Ready, Go," run to the blocks and pick one up, then run back to the starting line and place the block behind the line. Run and pick up the second block and run back across the starting line.

Rules: 1. Record the score as your time to the nearest one-tenth second. 2. Do not throw the blocks across the line.

If your scores are equal to or higher than the scores shown, you qualify for the Presidential Physical Fitness Award.

Sometimes it is easier to enjoy exercising when participating in an organized sport. You can play it smart by picking a sport that will keep you fit and develop coordination. Sports that develop muscles and endurance are swimming, football, short- and long-distance running, soccer, bicycling, and wrestling. Sports that develop coordination and agility are gymnastics, tennis, racquetball, squash, baseball, volleyball, basketball, diving, fencing, judo, and karate.

Even if you don't participate in a sport, you can improve your coordination in enjoyable ways. Throwing and catching a frisbee, for instance, is a great way to develop your hand and wrist movements. Kicking a footbag (Hacky Sack) also improves motion and coordination. Computer games are good for speeding up your reaction time and hand-eye coordination.

Gardner, Robert. *The Young Athlete's Manual.* New York: Julian Messner, 1985. **FURTHER READING**

12

Facing the Future

If you have decided to read this book, it is likely that you have already thought about becoming an astronaut before you picked it up. This book is designed to help start you off on a career as an astronaut, but some people do not decide what they want to do when they grow up until they have grown up. Other people know exactly what they want to do at a very early age. In between are the majority of people. These folks—and you may be one of them—would like to be something special but don't decide for sure until they are in college.

Even if you do not make up your mind now, you can still become an astronaut when you grow up. This book is about getting ready to be an astronaut, but it can also help you in other careers. The important thing is to learn to enjoy learning. If you develop good study habits and a good grasp of math and science, you will have more choices about what to do in the future than those who don't.

If you find something that interests you, go for it. Not every school or parent can take the time to help you out, so you must be prepared to create your own opportunities. Write letters, ask questions, read books, be active.

Remember, the future starts now!

Conversion Table

The metric system of measurement uses:
  meters for length
  grams for mass (weight at sea level)
  liters for volume

Some equivalent measurements:
  1 inch = 2.54 centimeters
  1 foot = 0.305 meters
  1 yard = 0.9144 meters
  1 mile = 1.609 kilometers
  1 pound = 0.454 kilograms
  1 quart = 0.946 liters
  1 centimeter = 0.3937 inches
  1 meter = 39.37 inches
  1 kilometer = 0.621 mile
  1 gram = 0.035 ounce
  1 kilogram = 2.20 pounds
  1 liter = 1.06 quarts

To convert U.S. customary units to metric, multiply by the factor indicated. For example:
  20 inches × 2.54 centimeters = 50.8 centimeters
  50 yards × 0.9144 meters = 45.7 meters

To convert metric units to U.S. customary units, divide by the factor. For example:
  500 kilometers ÷ 1.609 = 310 miles
  35 kilograms ÷ 2.20 = 11.36 pounds

Glossary

aeronautical engineer: an engineer who designs, develops, and tests aircraft or missiles

aeronautics: the science of travel outside of the earth's atmosphere

aerospace engineer: an engineer who designs, develops, and tests aircraft, missiles, rockets, or spacecraft

aerospace science: the study of material that can be used in aircraft, missiles, spacecraft, or satellites

airlock: a small room that allows pressure to be equalized between two areas

altitude: the distance above the surface of the earth

Apollo program: a series of missions to the moon that began in 1968. Both unpiloted and piloted missions were flown in the program, which ended in 1972.

asteroids: small bodies that orbit the sun but are too small to be planets. The largest known asteroid is about 600 miles in diameter.

astronaut: a person who travels in space (above the earth's atmosphere). Usually, this word is used to refer to an American space traveler.

astronomy: the science or study of the universe outside of the earth's atmosphere

astrophysics: the science or study of the physical properties of planets and other bodies in outer space. Astrophysics is a branch of astronomy.

atmosphere: a layer of gases surrounding a planet

attitude: the position of an aircraft or spacecraft relative to the earth

avionics: the electronic instruments and controls used to maneuver and keep track of an aircraft or spacecraft

cargo bay: the carrying space of the space shuttle. The cargo bay is unpressurized and can carry satellites for launching or spacelab modules.

commander: the astronaut in charge of a shuttle mission

communications satellite: a satellite in orbit around the earth that relays electronic information from one point on the surface to another

cosmonaut: an astronaut in the Soviet Union

de-orbit burn: a rocket engine firing that slows a spacecraft down, below the speed necessary to maintain an orbit

deployment: unloading the cargo of a spaceflight in space

docking: joining two spacecraft together in space

EMU (extravehicular mobility unit): the spacesuit that astronauts use when they are outside the shuttle. It is a self-contained life-support system.

ESA: European Space Agency

escape velocity: the speed necessary for an object to leave the gravitational field of a planet or moon

EVA (extravehicular activity): actions performed outside of a spacecraft

flare: a shuttle flight maneuver that pitches the nose up and slows the spacecraft

Gemini program: the second U.S. piloted rocket program. The first Gemini launch was in 1965, the last was in 1966.

geostationary orbit (also known as geosynchronous orbit): an orbit around the earth at an altitude of 22,300 miles (35,900 kilometers). At this height, an object orbits at the same speed as the earth and so remains above the same spot on earth.

g-force: a unit of gravity. One *g* equals the normal gravitational force on the earth's surface.

gravity: the force that every mass has, which attracts other masses

hardware: the mechanical and electronic parts of a computer

hypersonic: speeds above Mach 5 (five times the speed of sound)

Lagrange points: the locations between a planet and its moon where the gravitational forces of both are equal. There are five Lagrange points between the earth and the moon, but only two that are considered safe as a site for a future space colony.

launch control: the main control room and personnel that oversee the launch of a spacecraft

launch window: a period of time during a rocket or shuttle launch when the least amount of fuel will be used to reach a destination

Mach: a unit of speed. Mach 1 is the speed of sound, and Mach 2 is twice the speed of sound.

mass driver: an electromagnetic machine that can accelerate objects into space from the surface of the moon or an asteroid

Mercury program: the first U.S. piloted rocket program. The first Mercury launch was in 1961, and the last was in 1963.

micro-gravity: the condition of apparent weightlessness for objects in earth orbit. These objects are constantly falling forward around the earth and at the same time being pulled outward by centrifugal force. The two motions counteract each other except for a very small, unnoticeable effect called micro-gravity. Micro-gravity is often referred to as zero-gravity.

mission control: the main control room and personnel that oversee the mission operations and objectives of a spaceflight

mission specialist: an astronaut who assists in the deployment of shuttle cargo or other activities that are part of a shuttle mission

MMU (manned maneuvering unit): the backpack power device that astronauts use when they need to maneuver away from the shuttle

NASA (National Atmospheric and Space Administration): A department of the U.S. government that runs programs involved with space research and exploration

Nomex: a fiber made of synthetic materials that is very resistant to heat. It is used in some places on the outside skin of the space shuttle for insulation.

OMS (orbital maneuvering system): the rockets used to move the shuttle from one orbit to another and slow it down for reentry

orbit: the curved path that an object takes when rotating around another object

OV (orbital vehicle): the official name for a space shuttle

payload specialist: an astronaut who works on a specific shuttle experiment or payload. Payload specialists are not usually career astronauts.

pilot: the astronaut who is second in command of a shuttle flight and is trained to fly the spacecraft

Pioneer program: a U.S. program of unpiloted spacecraft. Pioneer probes have been sent to the Moon, Jupiter, Saturn, and other planets.

planetarium: a light projector that simulates stars, constellations, and planets in special domed theaters

radio astronomy: the use of radio-wave transmissions to study stars and other objects in space

RCS (reaction control system): the rockets used to change the attitude of the shuttle when it is in orbit, or move it for short distances

RMS (remote manipulator system): the remote-control arm that is used in the shuttle cargo bay

satellite: a natural or artificial body that orbits around a planet

simulator: a computer or mechanical device that mimics the feel and response of a piece of equipment, such as the manned maneuvering unit (MMU)

Skylab: a U.S. orbiting laboratory, which was launched in 1973. Several different groups of astronauts visited and worked in Skylab.

software: a set of programmed instructions for a computer

spacelab: a special module carried on some shuttle flights. It contains a laboratory for experiments in space.

space station: an orbiting space structure in which astronauts live and work

space telescope: a telescope in orbit around the earth

SRB (solid rocket booster): the reusable rocket that is used to launch the shuttle. Two SRBs are used for each launch.

STS (Space Transportation System): the official name of the space shuttle with the external fuel tank and the solid rocket boosters

thrust: the force developed in reaction to the firing of a rocket engine

zero-gravity: see micro-gravity

Index